PLAGUES

IN THE PALACE

BRADLEY BOOTH

Pacific Press® Publishing Association
Nampa, Idaho
Oshawa, Ontario, Canada
www.pacificpress.com

Designed by Randy Jamison
Cover art by Lars Justinen

Copyright © 2006 by
Pacific Press® Publishing Association
Printed in the United States of America
All rights reserved

Additional copies of this book are available by calling toll free
1-800-765-6955 or by visiting www.adventistbookcenter.com

ISBN: 0-8163-2143-4
ISBN13: 9780816321438

06 07 08 09 10 · 5 4 3 2 1

DEDICATION

To Aubie, my daughter, and Steve, my son.

When you were little children,

you were so much fun to tell stories to.

I pray that your children will be good listeners for you,

as you were for me.

Other books by Bradley Booth

The Prodigal

They Call Him the Miracle Man

CONTENTS

CHAPTER 1

Meshach stared at the colorful images painted on the walls of the long corridor. Rows of people, animals, and chariots in shades of yellow, red, and topaz splashed their way from one end of the hallway to the other. He just stood with mouth agape at the strangeness of it all.

The stone floor felt cool beneath his feet, and all about him stood statues and stone carvings of all kinds. Meshach had never been in this part of the palace before. In fact, at the moment, he wasn't really sure where he was. He was supposed to be delivering refreshments to the royal queen and her guests in the palace, but he must have taken a wrong turn somewhere.

Meshach listened carefully to muted voices echoing down the stony corridor. The voices sounded as if they were coming from a large vaulted chamber nearby.

Meshach felt excited that he should be asked to do such an important task. He was tall for his age and strong. He had average looks, with bronze skin, almond brown eyes, and a head of dark hair. But his pleasant smile made people stop and greet him when he walked down the hallways of the palace or when he came into a room.

Just recently Meshach had begun working with his father, Eli, a Hebrew slave in the bakery of the royal kitchens. Eli was a skilled baker, so his services were in great demand. Meshach knew his father was fortunate. Even for a slave, working in a bakery was much better than working on a construction crew building pyramids or temples. It could be hot in the bakery, but it was nothing like working in the broiling desert sun.

Meshach loved being with his father. His father was a big man with strong hands. Like Meshach, he had dark hair, and, like Meshach, he had a smile that lit up his face when he laughed. Eli was fun-loving and knew how to make work become a game. The two of them always laughed and joked when they were together, and sometimes his father even sang with his rich deep voice while they worked.

And Eli knew how to make the best bread around. The freshly baked bread always smelled so good when Meshach helped his father take the crusty round loaves from the ovens. Meshach loved to tear off pieces of the hot bread and pop them into his mouth.

But although Meshach liked working with his father in the palace kitchens, he didn't get to do it as often as he wanted. Now that Meshach was thirteen and no longer considered a boy, his father wanted him to learn how to read and write well. Then he could become a scribe.

His mother, Jerusha, was his tutor. Fortunately, she knew how to read and write and even do some calculations in math. Her father had been a scribe and had taught her well. Meshach knew it was unusual for a woman to have been given the chance to learn.

Meshach was a good student. Already he was getting pretty good with the letters he practiced using a wet clay tablet with a writing stick called a stylus. The letters formed words of an ancient language called Hebrew, the name used for Meshach's people. This form of writing had been used by Abraham, Isaac, and Jacob, but since the Hebrews had been in slavery for many generations, very few people could read and write the language anymore.

"I don't want my children growing up ignorant," Meshach's father had said more times than Meshach could remember. "You never know what God may call you to do with these skills someday. We're lucky that your mother can read and write. Many families are not so blessed." He would always smile and ruffle Meshach's hair when he said this, and although Meshach didn't like to study so much, he knew his father was right.

Meshach's father could read and write too. He should have been working full time as a scribe himself, but because he was such an excellent baker, Pharaoh's chief steward, Hatsuret, had insisted that he work in the bakery for the time being. Eli's skills as a scribe also came in handy when Hatsuret began having him keep the records up to date for all that was bought or sold in the kitchen.

Meshach hoped to be a good scribe one day, too—but today he didn't have to study. His mother couldn't teach him and his cousin, Asher, because her sister was having her third baby. Besides caring for her own family, Jerusha also served as a midwife for the Hebrew women in the neighborhood where Meshach lived.

It felt good to be free from classes for the day. Meshach was tired of sitting cross-legged on the floor for hours at a time copying the dark marks his mother wrote on a whitewashed clay-brick wall in their house. On days he didn't have to study, he would work with his father in the palace bakery, helping to make breads, cakes, and wafers for the palace meals.

Meshach continued wandering though the hallways of the palace looking for the chamber where Queen Tiye would be entertaining her guests. He had never been this far inside the royal palace. As he started down another long hallway, those muffled voices he had heard before sounded louder. Meshach walked along carefully as he carried the fresh bread, beer, and platter of melons and pomegranates. Meshach's father had told him to look for Saatet, chief of the palace servants, who had ordered the afternoon refreshments for the queen and some of her friends.

Meshach wrinkled his nose in disgust. Fresh bread tasted good, but he never had liked the warm beer that the royal kitchens brewed in large clay jars. After a while it would get frothy, and if it wasn't used up soon enough, it always developed a musty smell.

Everybody drank beer—men, women, and even children. It was the most common drink in Egypt, but that didn't change the way Meshach felt about it.

Suddenly Meshach caught sight of a small room tucked away at one end of the corridor. In the room was a window opening, and the voices he had been hearing were coming through it. Maybe the queen and her guests were in a chamber on the other side of the window. "You'll know you have arrived at Queen Tiye's chambers when you see filmy purple curtains hanging in the doorway," Eli had told him. "Her favorite color is purple."

Meshach didn't see the purple curtains he had been told to look for. Had he missed some passageway somewhere? His father had been quite specific. "You can't miss it. It's three corridors down from the large banquet hall with the pictures of sphinxes on the wall. Her chamber doors are the ones with the purple curtains."

Meshach had trembled with excitement at the responsibility of serving Queen Tiye. It wasn't every day that a Hebrew boy got to bring refreshments to the wife of the most powerful man in the world. Meshach stepped to the small window and peered through it. *Is this the chamber where I am supposed to deliver the bread and fruit?*

He nearly swallowed his tongue in surprise. In a large room below him Meshach could see golden furniture and green plants of every sort. Rich silk curtains of blues and reds gave the chamber a grandeur and elegance beyond anything Meshach had ever seen.

"Whew!" Meshach whistled to himself. Bronze-chested warriors were everywhere! They were tall and silent, and their spearheads and swords glimmered in the light of the sun streaming through small windows high in the white stone walls of the palace.

A narrow turquoise carpet with yellow fringes stretched down the center of the chamber. Meshach's eyes followed the length of it until it ended before a glistening white throne.

"Whoa, now! That's got to be ivory!" Meshach had to stop himself from shouting. "This is incredible! A throne overlaid with pure ivory! Wow! I've heard about stuff like this in stories father has told me, but I never thought I'd get to see it!"

Meshach's eyes wandered to the high vaulted ceiling supported by massive stone columns. He marveled at the tremendous size of the columns. And everywhere were chiseled and carved the likenesses of strange creatures, half-animal and half-man. He could clearly see carvings of Ra the sun god, with a human body but the head of a falcon. Then there was Apis, the black bull, and Bastet, the cat-headed god.

"What is this place?" Meshach gasped. "I must be at one of the royal audience chambers for the Pharaoh himself!" The fact that he had wandered so near an important room scared Meshach. *What if someone catches me watching from the small window? Will I be in trouble? Will I be dragged off and beaten? Perhaps put in prison?*

Meshach's common sense told him he should just find Queen Tiye's chambers and deliver the refreshments—but he didn't.

CHAPTER 2

Suddenly a whirl of activity unfolded below in the magnificent royal chamber. Dancers and acrobats exploded through filmy curtains hanging in doorways between the stone columns. They whirled and twirled their way up the carpeted approach to the throne. Jugglers raced to take their positions, and musicians began playing a haunting melody on flutes and stringed instruments.

Moments later a pompous man entered the chamber and took his place on the ivory throne. He was dressed in linen of the purest white, and a wide collar of beautiful turquoise and gold hung across his shoulders. Its shade of blue-green was as beautiful as the sparkling waters of the Great Sea. He wore ankle bands and arm bracelets of gold and a black wig beneath a heavily ornamented head piece.

"Wow!" Meshach caught his breath. "This must be Pharaoh Amenhotep himself, ruler of all Egypt!"

Meshach cringed as he said the words to himself. It hurt to think that his people, the Hebrews, were oppressed slaves in the pagan land of Egypt. *How could this have happened to God's chosen people?* It was a mystery to Meshach. *Do the Hebrews deserve slavery?* Meshach's father had told him that the Hebrew patriarch Jacob had come to Egypt with his children and grandchildren. There had been a worldwide famine at the time, and Egypt was the only place they could find food. As a gift from Pharaoh, Jacob's family had received some of the best land in the Nile Delta so they could pasture their flocks of goats, sheep, and cattle.

Of course that had been when Joseph, Jacob's son, was governor of all Egypt. That was an amazing story itself! Unfortunately, after Joseph died, a new pharaoh who had no respect for Joseph came to the throne. The new pharaoh, Thutmose, had claimed he didn't know of the good things Joseph had done for Egypt. He didn't care about the dreams Joseph had accurately interpreted that had saved Egypt from starvation. Joseph was remembered only as a barbarian foreigner from Canaan and inferior to the Egyptians. Or so the story went.

It didn't really matter anymore. The Hebrews were slaves in a foreign land now, and there was not much that could change that. Unless—unless of course one considered the promise. Meshach's father had told him many times that one day the Hebrews would all return to Canaan, the land of milk and honey. It was a promise from way back. They would all move to Shechem or Bethel, or one of the other places where the patriarch Jacob had originally lived with his twelve sons. Or maybe the Hebrew tribes would move to southern Canaan near Hebron, where Father Abraham had lived for so many years.

Of course there were thousands and thousands of Hebrews now, instead of the seventy family members that Jacob had brought with him to Egypt more than two hundred years before. Now they just might fill up the whole land of Canaan.

The old men in the Hebrew settlements of Goshen could tell good stories too. One tale they always told around the fires at night was about a cave at Hebron in the land of Canaan. All the important ancestors of the family had been buried in the cave. Father Abraham was buried there with his wife, Sarah. His son, Isaac, and Isaac's wife, Rebekah, were buried there too, and Leah and Jacob. Great-great-great-great-grandfather Jacob had died in Egypt, but before he died, he made his sons promise to take him back to Canaan to bury him in the legendary cave.

Meshach shivered as he thought about all those skeletons in one place. It made him feel creepy. They were his ancestors, though, and he knew they were an important part of his Hebrew heritage. The best parts of his family history had taken place in the land of Canaan.

Canaan seemed like a perfect home. That was where the family had lived for generations before they had decided to come to Egypt because of the famine. And even though Meshach had never been to Canaan, it seemed as if he belonged there too. He wished that he could go to Canaan and see all the sites for himself. In Canaan everything was supposed to be bigger and better. Meshach had heard that in some places the clusters of grapes grew so big, it took two men to carry them.

But were all these stories true, or were they just tales to be told around the fires at night? Could any place be perfect? Meshach frowned as he remembered that sometimes the old men also told of other things in Canaan that weren't so nice—dark, frightening tales of enormous fortresses filled with fierce giants. Surely they were just stories, but whenever Meshach thought about the giants in Canaan, he always shivered with fear.

Meshach shook off his fears of giants as he suddenly realized that something was happening in the chamber below him. The Pharaoh was dismissing the performers with a wave of his arm. That was all it took to make the dancers, jugglers, and musicians vanish as quickly as they had arrived.

All was still as a court crier announced the arrival of some visiting dignitary. Almost in reply, another procession glided down the carpeted walkway to kneel before the splendid throne. Through it all, Pharaoh Amenhotep remained on his throne, his face expressionless as the visitors knelt before him.

A few other important looking guests came and then went in quick succession. It seemed as if the Pharaoh was not interested in welcoming any of them, or in hearing what it was that they had come to say.

"He sure is grumpy!" Meshach whispered to himself. "I guess the royal court must be over for the day."

But the court crier called out yet again. Meshach continued to stare through the little window. Coming down the approach to the throne were two foreigners.

They don't look like anyone special to me, Meshach thought. No important looking officials walked before them, and there were no colorful robes. The only unique thing about them was their beards and the rather plain clothes they were wearing. They certainly looked like foreigners. Egyptians didn't wear beards.

One was a bit shorter than the other and carried a long shepherd's rod. Meshach couldn't really make out their faces because they marched into the room from under the window where he stood.

"What on earth do those men think they're doing in here?" muttered Meshach. "Look at them! They've got to know they're way out of their league dressed like that! This is the court of the great Pharaoh!" Meshach shook his head and grinned. "They won't last a minute before the honored Pharaoh Amenhotep, son of Ra, and ruler over all the land of the Nile!"

CHAPTER 3

Far below on the floor of the royal court, the two bearded visitors stood respectfully before Pharaoh.

"Not you two again!" barked an important looking official standing beside the throne. He appeared to be the Pharaoh's spokesman.

The visitor carrying the rod stepped forward and spoke in a voice so resonant that Meshach had no trouble hearing every word he said. "Amenhotep, great Pharaoh of all Egypt, we come before you as ambassadors of the Most High who rules the heaven and earth!"

The voice of the official began to drone out a response, as Meshach continued staring at the scene in the throne room below him. *Could it possibly be?* Meshach wondered. *Is this the pair of brothers that everyone has heard so much about?* Aaron was the speaker, the older of the two—Moses was the famous one. But what were they doing here?

Meshach's mind raced back to stories about Moses he had heard around the evening fires. Moses had been born under the oppressive government of Thutmose, the pharaoh ruling Egypt at that time. The court advisors had warned Thutmose that the number of Hebrew slaves was growing too large, that soon there would be more Hebrews in the land of Egypt than Egyptians themselves. Because of this, he had begun ordering a horrible thing—that all the Hebrew baby boys be killed by throwing them into the Nile. He hoped that this would help keep the Hebrew nation from becoming too strong.

Not surprisingly, Moses' mother had tried to keep Moses hidden from Pharaoh's death squad of soldiers sent out to execute the babies. She had somehow managed to hide Moses for three months, even though the

Egyptian soldiers had searched through the Hebrew settlement in Goshen every day. Finally she made a plan to save little Moses by building a basket out of reeds. She made the basket waterproof so that it would float and then hid Moses in it among the bulrushes along the riverbank.

Meshach smiled when he thought about how successful the plan had been. It had worked so well, in fact, that the baby Moses had been found and rescued from the Nile River by none other than Pharaoh's daughter, Hatshepsut. His basket was drifting along among the reeds when she discovered him. Since she could not have any children of her own, she had then adopted Moses to be raised as her very own son.

At first Hatshepsut had hired Jochebed, Moses' Hebrew mother, to care for Moses and raise him. However, when he was twelve years old, Moses went to live with Hatshepsut in the palace. And with that he had vanished from the Hebrew settlements into the life of royalty—gone forever from the streets and homes of his people.

That had been years ago.

Suddenly Meshach realized that Aaron was speaking to the Pharaoh again, and his words made Meshach tingle with excitement. "This is what Jehovah says to you, Amenhotep! 'Let My people go so that they can come apart to worship Me.' " Aaron didn't raise his eyes to look the Pharaoh in the face.

The court official looked at the two bearded brothers and smirked. "That's your request!" he snorted.

"Yes, most honored one. As before, we come to humbly make our request known to the great Pharaoh."

"But you have already heard the Pharaoh's decision. Why come again with the same request?"

Meshach peered intently at Pharaoh Amenhotep sitting on his ivory throne. It was almost as if the Pharaoh wanted to ignore the two visitors, and yet, at the same time, he was annoyed by them. Through it all, though, he had said not a word to the two brothers standing before him.

Aaron grasped his long rod tightly in his hand. "The Creator and Sustainer of all life has spoken, and we can only obey His command."

"Yes, Yes! We've heard all that," snapped the official as he stepped toward Aaron and Moses. "But Pharaoh will not change his mind! He has spoken—and his word is law!"

"Where are your official papers of authorization?" interrupted a scribe in a nasal tone. Holding a sheet of papyrus on a writing board and a reed pen, he stepped forward from behind Pharaoh's throne. "Your official documents?" he repeated in a businesslike manner, looking first at Aaron, and then at Moses. "Before we can go any further, we simply must have proof of your authorization for this visit. What territory or state do you represent, and—"

"Stupid!" hissed the court spokesman under his breath. "We already know what we need to know about these two fools!" He cleared his throat and continued, "Now! Since you men have nothing more to say that we don't already know, you may show yourselves out. Your audience with the Pharaoh is ended."

"Please!" Aaron took a step forward. "You have not considered the consequences of refusing to let Israel go. Jehovah is not one to be trifled with. When He—"

"Enough!" The majestic Pharaoh rose from his ivory throne, interrupting Aaron. His patience ended as he stood to his feet and glared at the two visitors. "I have heard enough! Words mean nothing to me!" His eyes flashed in anger. "You come here with nothing to represent your God—not that it would make any difference! You have no gifts, no royal papers, and you certainly have no respect for me, the great Pharaoh Amenhotep! If you did, you would never come here making such demands!"

The ruler's face was stern, and his voice was harsh. "On your knees, faces to the floor!" He ordered. "You will reverence me, do you hear! You will give me the worship and respect that is mine!" He spat the words out as if they were bitter poison.

Aaron glanced at Moses, and then at the Pharaoh. "I'm sorry your majesty. We worship Jehovah alone—we owe no worship to anyone but Him."

Amenhotep glared at the two brothers standing before him. "And I owe no allegiance to this—this Jehovah God, whoever He is!" he roared. "I have never heard of Him before, and I don't care to know Him now!"

Aaron looked at the floor, but Moses refused to give ground to the Pharaoh. He lifted his face with dignity as he stared Pharaoh Amenhotep full in the face. Clutching Aaron's arm, Moses impatiently pushed his brother toward the throne. "Say something!" Moses muttered under his breath.

It was obvious that Aaron was doing all the talking, and Meshach wondered why.

Aaron glanced at Moses again, hesitated, and then turned to the Pharaoh. "Pharaoh Amenhotep, ruler of all Egypt, if you will not obey the voice of Jehovah, then there is little more for us to say."

To Meshach it sounded as if Aaron was giving up, and yet there was the hint of something more to come. "As the Most High God lives, we do have one more message for you. So that you and all Egypt may know that Jehovah has all power in heaven and earth, we bring you this sign."

Aaron then lifted his rod in the air and threw it to the floor, where it clattered about on the polished marble surface.

CHAPTER 4

Meshach jumped back in surprise. To his amazement, and everyone's in the courtroom, the rod on the marble floor instantly turned into a poisonous cobra. Its golden scales glinted in the light of the afternoon sun filtering through the small windows high in the courtroom walls. Its long black tongue darted out of its mouth as it turned this way and that, surveying the room and everyone in it.

The room buzzed with excitement as everyone backed away from the serpent. Pharaoh Amenhotep himself stood up and stepped to the side of his throne. His face, however, remained calm and showed no fear.

"Did I see what I think I just saw!" Meshach gasped. He rubbed his eyes and stared down at the courtroom floor. The cobra turned toward the steps of Pharaoh's throne and began to slither slowly up the steps one by one.

"I must be dreaming!" Meshach exclaimed. "The cobra looks real—but—but it can't be!" He glanced from one side of the courtroom to the other searching for an explanation of some kind. "A rod can't become a snake," he muttered. "Wood is wood, and no matter what magic anyone uses, there's just no way that—" Meshach stopped short. He squinted, and then scratched his head.

This was some sort of miracle—there was no doubt about that! Had Moses and Aaron used some secret power to make the rod look as if it had become a cobra? Meshach had heard about the powers of sorcery that the high priests often used. The black arts of magic they practiced were feared by the Egyptians, but Moses and Aaron were men of God. They wouldn't use the powers of darkness, would they?

Moses certainly knew about the magic. After all, he had grown up in the royal palace where such sorcery was practiced. He had sat at the feet of all the great men of Egypt, and they had no doubt showed him many strange and mysterious things. Many of these teachers were priests in the temples dedicated to the gods Egyptians worshiped. They would have seen to it that Moses knew all about Ra, the sun god, and Osiris, god of the Nile.

And these priests would have probably tried to teach Moses about other secret arts of Egypt, such as astrology, which was a study of the stars. They would probably have wanted him to learn how to channel the spirits, which was a way of communicating with the spirit world.

Meshach frowned. Had Moses gotten mysterious powers from the royal magicians and sorcerers who had been his personal tutors when he was a student in Egypt? Or had he gotten them from Jehovah?

"In the name of Jehovah who is the source of all life, once more we ask that you let Israel go to worship Him in peace." Meshach realized that Aaron was speaking again.

Amenhotep continued staring at the cobra, but he didn't flinch. Finally, he whispered something to a court scribe standing at his side. Without a word the scribe turned and left the courtroom.

Meshach looked at Moses and Aaron, and then at Pharaoh. Was the standoff over? Had the two brothers won their case? Would Pharaoh let Moses and Aaron take the Hebrew slaves and go worship Jehovah?

Within minutes Meshach had his answer as a group of temple priests walked into the throne room and past the rows of tall stone columns. The priests' heads were shaved, and they were all bare chested. Not a hair could be seen on their bodies—even their eyebrows had been shaved. They dressed in the uniform of all priests—a white linen kilt hung from their waists. One priest wore a golden collar around his neck, and Meshach wondered if he might be the high priest. He looked to be more important than the others.

The priest with the golden collar quietly approached Pharaoh Amenhotep, who was now standing behind the throne to one side. Flickering torches had been lit by the palace guards to keep the cobra at a distance, and the flames made little wisps of black smoke curl across the Pharaoh's worried face.

Pharaoh Amenhotep and the high priest carried on a whispered conversation for a few minutes, and then the high priest returned to his place among the other priests.

What will happen next? Meshach wondered *Will the priests kill the poisonous cobra on the steps to the throne?* Meshach doubted it. Cobras were considered sacred to Egyptian worship. *Will the high priest use his evil enchantments to cast a spell on Moses and Aaron? Will he order the palace guards to take Moses and Aaron away in chains?* Meshach realized it was even possible that the two brothers could be executed for daring to defy Pharaoh.

Meshach watched as the high priest stepped forward and held his own rod in his outstretched hand. Meshach knew the staff was a type of divining rod. He had seen noblemen carrying them from time to time and had asked his father how such rods were used. Meshach's father had said the rods were a sign of a man's power and authority in the territory where he ruled.

The high priest's rod was more fancy than Aaron's rod. It was made of ivory with silver trimmings on it.

Will the high priest use his rod to push or pull the cobra out of the courtroom? Meshach wondered. *Will someone get bitten and possibly die?* The cobra was very large—it had to be deadly poisonous!

But on the other hand, is the cobra real? And if not, is it still dangerous? After all, it had been a rod only moments before. By now Meshach was so mixed up, he didn't know what to think.

But if Meshach was surprised at what had already happened, he was in for a bigger surprise. What happened next made the hair on the back of his neck stand up.

CHAPTER 5

With a sudden flourish, the high priest dropped his rod to the floor, where it rolled around on the marble's shiny surface. And then one by one the rest of the priests threw their rods to the floor. Meshach counted them as they landed on the floor—there were seven in all. Some were made of gold, others were polished ebony wood with jeweled trim. Each rod represented the rank of the priest in the temple of the god where he served.

And then, amazingly, as all the rods hit the floor they too became serpents. Meshach gasped as they coiled and uncoiled their scaly bodies and then began to slowly advance toward Aaron's cobra now on the bottom step to Pharaoh's throne. Aaron's serpent was bigger than them all, but it was definitely outnumbered.

"Hey!" Meshach muttered under his breath. "This isn't fair! Seven to one isn't exactly fair odds, and these priests are sorcerers besides! They're using black magic!"

The seven serpents had now surrounded the big cobra in the center and fanned out, waiting to see what his next move would be. Suddenly with a lightning-quick jab, Aaron's cobra lashed out at its nearest attacker. Its deadly fangs sank deep into the neck of the smaller snake as the two of them rolled off the step and onto the smooth polished floor. They struggled together for a few moments until the smaller one lay limp.

Meshach found himself cheering for Aaron's cobra. "One down and six to go." In amazement Meshach watched as the super serpent attacked and killed each of the smaller serpents. And then, something even stranger happened. Aaron's large cobra began to slowly swallow the dead bodies of the smaller serpents. One by one he ate them, head first, until they were all gone.

When it was all over, everyone just stood looking at the large cobra stretched out at the foot of Pharaoh's throne. It was no larger or fatter than before it had eaten the other seven serpents. Aaron's cobra continued looking this way and that, its black tongue darting in and out as though it were contemplating its next move. Not a whisper could be heard in the courtroom.

But when Aaron reached out his hand and seized the cobra by the tail, everyone gasped in terror and then gasped again in surprise when they saw that the rippling body of the cobra had again become a wooden rod in Aaron's hand.

Pharaoh Amenhotep stood brooding over the scene, his shoulders slumping in the late afternoon shadows of the courtroom. He seemed to be struggling to decide what he should do with this demonstration of power. It was obvious that the power in Aaron's rod was stronger than the magic any of the priests could muster.

Moses and Aaron looked at Pharaoh confidently. "Now will you let the slaves go?" Aaron asked.

Pharaoh straightened up and shuddered as though he were trying to shake off the memory of what he had just witnessed.

He looked at the temple priests, and then at his court advisors before turning to Moses. "No! I will not!" he scowled. His eyes were cold, and his hooked nose and high cheekbones gave his unsmiling face a defiant look. "Now get out!" he ordered as he returned to his throne and sat down. "I have a country to run!"

Aaron shrugged his shoulders. "Very well, then—we'll go. However, I can promise you that we will return with words of judgment from Jehovah, words that you will not be pleased to hear."

Amenhotep stood up from his throne and sternly pointed to the tall doors standing open at the courtroom entrance. "Leave my presence!" he shouted.

Meshach straightened his back. He couldn't believe his ears! "Can you believe that!" he muttered. "Aaron turns a shepherd's rod into a cobra, and

Pharaoh says he's unimpressed. Aaron's serpent eats up all the other serpents, and the Pharaoh tells Moses and Aaron to go home." Meshach shook his head slowly. "The Pharaoh has lost his mind!"

As Moses and Aaron turned to go, Meshach suddenly remembered where he was and what he was supposed to be doing. He looked down at the large tray of food sitting on the floor beside him. The bread was no longer warm, and the melons had begun to dry. Worst of all, Meshach still had no idea where Queen Tiye's chambers were.

As Meshach stepped out into the main corridor, he met a servant girl coming toward him. "Excuse me, could you tell me where Queen Tiye is taking her afternoon refreshments?" Meshach felt embarrassed, and he knew his face was turning red, but he had to find the room. He had been keeping the queen and her guests waiting too long already.

"Down around the corner and two doors to the right," the servant girl replied. "The curtains in the doorway are—"

"I know, I know!" Meshach interrupted. "Purple curtains! I can't miss 'em, or so I've been told."

He turned away quickly and hurried down the corridor. As he turned the corner, he could see the purple curtains ahead—now he could finally deliver the refreshments. But as Meshach neared the doorway, Saatet stepped out into the corridor, his hands on his hips. And if looks could have killed, Meshach would have been dead on the floor.

CHAPTER 6

"What has been keeping you?" Saatet hissed, pointing a bony finger in Meshach's face.

Meshach hung his head. What had he been thinking when he stayed so long to watch the battle of the serpents? Of course Saatet was wondering where Meshach had been, and of course he wasn't happy at being made to wait. After all, he was in charge of all the servants and their duties in the palace estate!

"I—I'm sorry!" Meshach stammered, his face turning red. "I got lost on the way, and I—"

"I'll say you did!" snapped the middle-aged man. "Probably playing along the way! Boys!" Saatet glowered at Meshach.

Meshach wondered that Saatet hadn't had a major breakdown long before. He was not a strong man. His head was nearly bald, and his frail shoulders were stooped. It seemed that nothing could make him smile. And always he was agitated with the things that people did or didn't do. If Meshach hadn't been wondering how he was going to be punished for making Saatet wait, he might have had time to feel sorry for the man.

"I'll deal with you later, young man! You can be sure that your father is going to hear about this!" he barked.

And Meshach was sure his father would. Saatet rarely let a mistake slide. Meshach didn't mind getting punished for a mistake, but he felt sorry for his father. His father's reputation in the royal palace was important, and Meshach didn't want his father to suffer for the mistake of his careless son.

"Yes, Saatet." Meshach hesitated. "Is there anything more I can do for you?"

"No, I think you've done quite enough! Now, get back to the kitchen! Maybe you can stay out of trouble there and get something done for a change!"

The words stung, but Meshach knew Saatet was right. Meshach was probably better suited for work in the kitchen. He was just too easily distracted to be performing duties out and about on the palace estate.

Meshach grinned in spite of his mistake. As much as he liked going to the far corners of the palace complex and meeting new people, he liked being with his father more. In the kitchens Meshach wouldn't have to worry so much about doing the wrong thing at the wrong time. His father understood that he was not much more than a boy.

As he turned to go, Meshach caught sight of a familiar face down the corridor. It was Seti, an Egyptian boy who also worked in the royal kitchens. Seti made a face and pointed at Meshach. He started laughing and then ducked out of sight. Meshach didn't like Seti much, but what could he do about it? Seti was always making fun of Meshach. He was a year older than Meshach, and bigger and stronger too.

Seti worked with his mother, helping to make the beer everyone in the palace drank. Maybe that was another reason Meshach didn't like Seti. He always smelled of warm beer.

Meshach hoped he didn't have to meet Seti again today. Seti made him nervous because he was always bragging about how superior the Egyptians were compared to the Hebrews. Meshach didn't want to admit it, but in a way, Seti was right. The Egyptians did rule the world, and the Hebrews were their slaves.

When Meshach arrived back in the kitchen, his father looked up from the bread dough he was kneading in a stone trough. "Well, my son, I see you finally made it back. You must have found something interesting to do." He winked at Meshach as he threw the ball of dough onto one of the wooden tables, cut it into smaller pieces, and then began shaping the lumps of dough into flat circles. He worked quickly as he placed them on a wooden board, and then slid the board into the clay oven at one end of the long kitchen.

Eli's words found their mark, and Meshach hung his head again with embarrassment. "Yes, Father—I mean—no. I mean, I did find something that distracted me, but I'm late because I lost my way, too." Meshach looked around him at the other workers in the kitchen, and then lowered his voice. "I couldn't find Queen Tiye's chambers, and then I heard voices and discovered a small window overlooking one of the royal courtrooms, and—"

"And you saw the famous brothers, Aaron and Moses, seeking an audience with Pharaoh Amenhotep?"

Meshach's mouth dropped open as he stared at his father.

A slight smile played around the corners of Eli's mustache and beard. He stoked the kitchen fires with some lumps of black bitumen pitch and then paused in his work to take a long drink from a clay jar of water nearby.

Eli wiped the water from his mouth with the back of his arm. He usually worked in the kitchen bare chested and barefoot and wore only a white loincloth around his hips and thighs. The kitchen was almost always hot, and sweat never stopped running down his face and chest.

Meshach continued to stare at his father until Eli's face broke into a smile. "Word travels quickly around here, Son. Most information from the palace passes through the kitchen."

Meshach looked a little bit disappointed. "Then you already know about how Aaron's rod became a cobra and ate up all the other serpents in the courtroom that were rods before the priests threw them on the floor?" Meshach stopped to catch his breath.

Eli smiled and laid his hand on Meshach's shoulder. "That's all right, Son. You were there, and that's more than I can say for myself."

"I suppose so," Meshach grew quiet, "but Father, I don't know what to think. I know what I saw, but I don't understand what it meant."

"What do you mean?" Eli leaned against the wall to rest for a moment.

"Well—Aaron changed his rod into a serpent, and then all the priests changed their rods into serpents." Meshach scratched his head. "Did they all use the same power? Were they using the powers of evil, or, maybe, was it Jehovah's power?"

"That's a good question." Eli handed Meshach a small clay cup of water. "The answer is probably quite simple. I would say—both."

Meshach took a long drink from the cup. "Both? But how can that be?"

"Well, Aaron was using the power of Jehovah, and the priests were using the power of the evil one."

"But, how do we know which was which? I mean, all the serpents looked real, and all of them made the hair stand up on the back of my neck."

"Meshach, Jehovah would never give that kind of power to pagan priests. The Pharaoh and the priests don't serve Jehovah. They don't even know who He is. They would have to get their power from the dark forces of Egyptian black magic."

Eli smiled. "On the other hand, why would Aaron and Moses use the power of the evil one? Why should they, when they already have the power of the universe at their fingertips?" Eli paused. "There were two forces working in that courtroom today, Meshach, and I think it is obvious to you which force won."

Eli shook his head and chuckled. "What I would have given to see the expressions on the faces of Pharaoh Amenhotep and his group of priests!" He lowered his voice as he leaned toward Meshach. "Was it good to see the proud Pharaoh humbled?"

Meshach nodded his head quickly and smiled too. "It was good, Father, but the Pharaoh didn't react the way I thought he would."

"And how did you expect him to react?"

"Well, I guess I thought he would be impressed at the way Aaron's rod changed into a cobra."

"And?"

"And—I thought Pharaoh would let our people go and worship Jehovah as Aaron and Moses asked."

Eli laughed, "Oh, ho, Meshach. I can see that you have much to learn." He lowered his voice again. "Pharaoh Amenhotep is a hard man—a cruel and heartless ruler. I know the Egyptians think of him as a god, but we Hebrews see him only as a brutal tyrant." Eli's eyes narrowed to slits and his voice grew serious. "Nothing is as dear to Pharaoh as having power over others, and I believe he would do anything to keep it—and I mean anything!"

Meshach studied his father's face. He wondered what other stories his father could tell him about the royal court and the Pharaoh who ruled it.

Almost in answer to Meshach's thoughts, Eli added, "I could tell you things about this man's reign that you would never believe, even if you saw them and heard them for yourself!" Eli glanced cautiously around the kitchen at the other workers who were busy with their own tasks. "But it would not be wise to tell you much," he added, "and certainly not here. The walls have ears, my son."

Meshach laughed right out loud. He could just imagine ears fastened to the walls of the long narrow kitchen—ears that heard every word he said, even if he whispered them.

CHAPTER 7

Meshach sat cross-legged on the floor of their one-room mud-brick home. It was time for the evening meal. As the meal was being prepared, he watched the small charcoal oven make weird shadows on the wall.

The meal had been set in the center of a woven rug made of goats' hair. It felt soft under Meshach's feet. A large clay pot of pottage sat in the center of the rug, and a platter of flat round bread sat beside it. Meshach licked his lips at the smell of savory lentils, garlic, and fresh bread.

Meshach's mother, Jerusha, was the best cook around. As was the custom, she and Kezia would serve the men and boys first, and then eat later, separately from the men. However, they all raised their eyes together toward heaven for the evening's blessings. That was a custom they all took part in, even if men and women did eat separately.

Meshach loved his family. His mother looked young for her age, but Meshach knew she worked too hard. Besides caring for her family, she was also a midwife. Often she stayed out all night caring for the women who were giving birth.

Chilion, Meshach's younger brother, was ten and smaller than many boys his age. He was quiet and serious, and there wasn't a day that passed when he wasn't bringing something interesting home to study. Sometimes it was a leaf or a strange rock. Sometimes it was a locust. One day he even brought home a small wooden contraption he had made that could fly. It had flat strips of wood that stuck out straight on either side, and when he tossed it into the air, it floated for quite a distance.

And then there was Kezia, Meshach's older sister. Like her mother, she was pretty with long dark hair. Meshach knew it wouldn't be long before young men in the Hebrew settlement would be asking for her hand in marriage. She was only fifteen, but already she could do everything that grown women could do.

Meshach was proud to be a part of this family, but he wondered how long things would stay as they were. He had a strange feeling in the pit of his stomach that somehow, very soon, everything was about to change. Now that Moses had come back, Meshach was sure their whole world was about to be turned upside down.

Meshach dipped a piece of bread into the large pot of lentils and garlic, and then looked at his father. "Tell me more about Moses, Father."

Eli glanced at Meshach before taking a drink of water from the clay cup at his side. "Hmmm, Moses—now, that is a man with an interesting story."

Meshach sat up straighter. "Father, now that Moses has returned to Egypt, I was hoping that you might know more about where he's been all these years. I mean, he did disappear for a long time. What was he doing?"

"Good question," Eli nodded with a twinkle in his eye.

"That's the problem," Meshach replied eagerly. "I've got so many questions, but—but I feel like I'm not supposed to ask them. I mean, it's as if Moses is carrying a big secret with him, and now after what happened at the court today, he seems even more mysterious to me."

Eli put his hand on Meshach's shoulder. "I couldn't agree with you more, Son." He paused and looked at Meshach. "You're becoming a man, so we can talk plainly. It's true, now that Moses has returned, we have more information than we've had in years. You see, no one knew much for the longest time—not even his family. He just disappeared into thin air, it seemed."

Eli paused and looked toward the open doorway. "You never know who might be listening, Meshach—I'm sure Pharaoh Amenhotep has spies living here in Goshen among us. Some of the spies are probably even Hebrews. I think that here at home we are fairly safe, though."

Meshach's father rubbed his full belly comfortably and sighed. He leaned back against the rough brick wall and watched the wisps of smoke curling upward from the embers of the charcoal oven that had cooked their supper.

"Moses was educated by the best that Egypt had to offer," Eli began. "He was given every opportunity under the direction of the master scribe who was in charge of all the tutors for the children in the royal family. Detu was his name, and they say he was a genius. According to all the accounts I've heard, he immediately saw the potential in the young boy Moses. Moses was only twelve when he moved into the palace, but already Detu could see his potential greatness.

"And Moses did do well. So well, in fact, that it soon became obvious that he would need other teachers more skilled in the subjects of trigonometry, hieroglyphics, and government. He also became skilled in the latest of weapons and warfare. They say that as Moses grew older, there wasn't a man in Pharaoh's personal guard or the special forces of his army who could beat Moses or outwit him. Not with javelin, sword, or bow. And no one could ride better than he."

Eli smiled. "Not surprisingly, he eventually became a general in the Pharaoh's army, and, as expected, he became a successful military leader. He fought in the battles of Upper Egypt near the border of Cush and also up north in the land of Canaan. And when he always came home victorious, there were parades in the streets of all the royal cities of Egypt. Everywhere people celebrated! Moses, the military genius, had come home."

Eli paused to stretch his legs. "By now Moses was the most famous man in all the land of Egypt—and the most popular. He was a favorite at court, and his adopted mother, Queen Hatshepsut, was pushing for him to become the next pharaoh. This was exciting news for all the Hebrews in Egypt. It fit in perfectly with the prophecies among our people that said a deliverer would come someday and free us from slavery." Eli turned and winked at Meshach. "And of course many were convinced that Moses might be the one. After all, he was himself a Hebrew."

Meshach squirmed with excitement as every part of the story unfolded. He could hardly make himself sit still to listen.

"For years Jehovah has sent his messengers among us," Eli continued. "We call them the seers, and they have prophesied deliverance for our people."

"Wow!" Meshach's eyes were bright. "You mean, deliverance through someone like Moses?"

"That's right."

"And then good times can begin again, and we can all go back to Canaan?"

"Well, yes, but of course there are some things that we have been told we must do, too, as Jehovah's people." Eli took another drink of water from his clay cup. "According to the seers, we must be faithful to our heritage. As far back as Great-great-great-grandfather Joseph, we have been urged to be true to the God of Abraham, Isaac, and Jacob."

"Faithful?" Meshach asked. "In what ways?"

"Faithful to keep Jehovah's holy Sabbath—and not worship idols. We are to worship only the one true God. And we are supposed to eat only certain animals. Much of what the Egyptians eat is not fit for the human body, you know." Eli sighed and his shoulders slumped a little in the gathering darkness. "It's hard for our people, living among pagans in a foreign land. I'm afraid many of the Hebrews have been unfaithful in obeying God's commands."

Meshach looked puzzled. "I don't get it," he said. "I know our people haven't always been faithful and everything, but after all, they are slaves. I mean, why didn't Moses just rise up and set the slaves free when he had a chance? If he had done that, then the Hebrews could have left Egypt, and we would all be in Canaan now, being faithful to Jehovah and doing all the things He wants us to do."

"Good point, Son. Good point." Eli smiled at Meshach's impatience. "That's the next part of the story." Eli tousled Meshach's dark head of hair. "Of course, as you know, Moses didn't set the slaves free. Something did happen, though, that changed things for Moses here in Egypt. It happened one afternoon as he was making rounds in his chariot.

"He was on an inspection tour of the building sites, and he saw an overseer beating a slave. The slave was a small man, and he was huddled on the ground begging for mercy. It didn't seem to matter to the Egyptian over-seer. They're a mean bunch, you know. Anyway, in spite of the poor slave's cries, the overseer continued to beat him again and again with a whip."

Eli paused and raised his eyebrows. "Now remember, Moses was a He-brew by birth, no matter where he grew up—so you can imagine how he must have felt as he witnessed the slave being beaten."

"I know how I'd feel," Meshach chimed in.

"Me too," Eli nodded. "I don't think I could just stand by and watch. Anyway, as the story goes, Moses was so upset at seeing the slave being beaten, that he jumped down from his chariot and grabbed the whip from the overseer."

"Really!" Meshach's eyes grew big.

"That's right, and then there was a struggle between the two of them."

"The two of them began to fight? Moses and the overseer?" Meshach couldn't believe his ears.

"That's right," Eli chuckled. "Now, overseers are typically quite strong. The government usually picks big men to manage the slaves. They've got to be tough. But of course Moses was strong too. In fact, because of Moses' great strength, he overpowered the overseer and actually ended up killing him."

Meshach couldn't believe his ears. Moses, the great man of God, was a murderer? Meshach had never imagined that such a thing could be. Was it possible? Were there other things from Moses' past that would surprise people? Were there other secrets waiting to be discovered?

CHAPTER 8

Meshach stared at his father. "Moses killed the overseer? I never heard that part before."

"Lots of people haven't," Eli added. "The story is a couple generations old. Maybe people think the whole thing is just a folktale. Who can say? Anyway, it did happen, and it was a terrible tragedy. At first, no one in the royal household would believe it, because Moses hid the body in the sand, but eventually word got out. You know how bad news gets out—it always finds a way."

Eli grew solemn as he told this part. "I think one of the reasons it shocked everyone so much was that no one expected it. Moses was such a favorite in the royal court and among the common people, too."

"But Father," Meshach's voice became softer. "Wasn't Moses just trying to help the poor slave? He shouldn't have killed the overseer, but he was part of the royal family. He could do what he wanted, couldn't he? And the Hebrews would at least be glad, wouldn't they? After all, he was helping one of them."

"You would think so," Eli replied, "but you've got to remember that no one really knew who he was anymore. Most doubted that they could trust someone who had lived in the palace his whole life."

Meshach frowned. "This doesn't make sense, Father! I mean, didn't our people see what he was trying to do?" Meshach shook his head in wonder. "This was their chance! The Hebrew slaves could have risen up and over-thrown the Egyptians! Why didn't they? There were enough of them—they could have if they had wanted to, couldn't they?"

"They could have. Maybe."

"What do you mean, 'maybe'? There are more of us than there are Egyptians."

"Well, it's true, we are many, but we aren't trained to fight. We don't have the weapons, and we would probably lack the courage and discipline to fight a real war, and that's what it would take." Eli's raised his finger. "However, I have my own ideas about why things went the way they did."

"You do?" Meshach looked at his father in surprise.

Eli nodded his head. "You see, I think Moses was beginning to realize that maybe he was the one who was supposed to deliver his people." Eli paused. "But, I also think it might not have been Jehovah's time for him to do the job. God's ways are not always our ways, you know."

"I've heard that one before." Meshach shook his head in disbelief. "But it's sad. Our people could have been free by now—it seems like such a terrible waste!"

"It does, doesn't it?" Eli sighed. "It's sad—not many people talk about it anymore—maybe they want to forget what was and what could have been. Anyway, somehow or other, the story has grown old. Hardly anyone speaks of it now." Eli's voice wavered.

Meshach thought about the things his father had told him as he watched the faint shadows from the charcoal oven dance across his father's face. "But, Father," Meshach kept on, "I don't understand. Wasn't Moses the son of the queen? Wasn't he the crown prince? Couldn't he have just freed the slaves, if he wanted? I mean, he was going to be the next pharaoh!"

"It would seem like that, wouldn't it?" Eli nodded. "It's true, there was no male heir to the throne. All of the pharaohs at that time had no boys—only girls. Moses probably did seem like the logical one to be the next pharaoh."

Eli straightened his legs to stretch them again. "But, Son, you must understand—there were many in Pharaoh's court who were not happy that Moses, a Hebrew, was allowed to enjoy such a high place in the family of the Pharaoh. If it hadn't been for the queen, the priests of Egypt would have seen to it that Moses would never be ruler in Egypt. In fact, there were many just waiting for him to make a mistake so that they could get rid of him—and now, of course, he had made that mistake. A huge one."

"So what happened then?"

"Well, Moses knew exactly what he had to do. From that point on he would be considered an enemy of the throne. His very life would be in danger if he remained in Egypt."

Meshach took a deep breath. "So he ran away?"

"Exactly. Now, until recently no one really knew what had happened or where Moses had gone. He just disappeared. Some thought that maybe he was killed by an angry relative. Others thought that Pharaoh had him executed for the murder, but that was later proven to be just a rumor. Many guessed that he must have gone into exile, but no one knew for sure. It was as if he had vanished into thin air."

Meshach's face grew sad. "So, I guess, along with the disappearance of Moses went everyone's hopes of a deliverer?"

"That's right, and he's been gone all these years—it must be—some forty years now, at least."

Meshach looked around the small room at the other family members. Chilion and Kezia had fallen asleep on the rug, and Mother was dozing too. Only the sound of a few dogs barking in the streets broke the evening's stillness.

The little fire in the charcoal oven had nearly burned itself out now. Meshach tossed enough fuel on the coals to keep it burning until morning. He turned to his father once more.

"Forty years. That's a long time, Father, and now he suddenly shows up? What's he been doing all these years? I mean, where was he all this time?"

"Well, for the last several years we've been hearing stories from the east, rumors about a desert chieftain living among the shepherds of Midian. Traveling merchants spoke of him as a great warlord, not so much because of the battles he won, but because of the way he brought peace to the tribes where he lived."

Meshach smiled. "And you think this warlord was Moses?"

"I know he was," Eli answered with a smile.

"So, now this warlord shows up demanding that Pharaoh let our people go?"

Eli nodded. "It looks like it, but that doesn't mean that Pharaoh will listen." He frowned and then sighed again. "The next few months are not going to be easy for us."

Meshach's face grew serious. "What do you mean, Father? If our people are set free, won't that be a good thing?"

"Of course it will be, but you don't think Pharaoh is going to let the slaves go without a struggle, do you?"

Meshach yawned and then closed his tired eyes. He hadn't thought of that. He just knew that there were a lot more Hebrews than Egyptians. Lots more. Some said there were hundreds of thousands more.

Meshach stared at the coals of fire now barely flickering. "Father, you know so much about Moses. I've never heard most of the stories you told me here tonight. Where did you hear them?"

Eli smiled again in the darkness. "Well, Son, I guess I do have somewhat of an edge on the rest of you. You see, I have been spending time at cousin Nadab's house for the last several days. Aaron has been there several times, and I have had a chance to talk with him personally about all this. We're all from the tribe of Levi," Eli added as he nudged Meshach. "You and I, Nadab and his brothers—and of course Aaron and Moses."

"Wow!" was all Meshach could say. It was too much information for a tired boy to handle.

Later Meshach lay on his reed mat looking up at the stars. Often he slept outside on the rooftop of their mud brick home. It was cooler up there. Thousands of Hebrew families lived like Meshach's family did—in one-room dwellings on the outskirts of Tanis in lower Egypt. Tanis was a royal city, and it was also where many Hebrew slaves worked building storehouses, temples, and monuments for the Pharaoh.

Meshach liked looking up at the night stars. It made him feel close to nature and Jehovah. Looking at all those stars made him feel small, but it also gave him a sense of peace. It made him feel good that the same God who had created the stars had also created him, a Hebrew boy in a nation of slaves in the land of Goshen. Meshach wasn't sure just what Jehovah would do next, but things were getting pretty exciting.

Were Moses and Aaron on the verge of doing something really great? Could Jehovah still use Moses, these many years later after he had been exiled for murder? Would the two brothers be the ones to finally lead a revolt of the Hebrews and bring an end to their slavery? Could they really pull it off with cruel Pharaoh Amenhotep on the throne?

Meshach could only wonder how this would all come about—was there something the Hebrew slaves needed to be doing first? Was deliverance going to come when the Hebrews began to live good lives and obey Jehovah's commands? That didn't seem likely. Meshach was glad to be living in a family where Jehovah was loved and obeyed, but not many Hebrew families knew much about Father Abraham's One True God anymore.

A warm wind blew in off the desert from the east as Meshach finally closed his eyes. He tingled with excitement as he remembered the events of the day. Jehovah, the God of the universe, was about to do big things for His people, and Moses had arrived in Egypt to be a part of it. Meshach could feel it in his bones, and he wanted to be there when it all happened. It was the most exciting feeling he had ever had.

CHAPTER 9

The sun's early morning rays slanted in through the open doorway of the royal kitchens as Meshach slid another batch of bread into the clay brick ovens. As always, whenever he could, Meshach came to the kitchens to work with his father. Today, again, Meshach's mother, Jerusha, could not teach the boys their reading and writing lessons. Again some of the mothers in Goshen needed her help.

Meshach was only too glad to have another day away from his studies. Working in the kitchens was hot, but Meshach knew it was better than working outside on Pharaoh's building projects. There the temperatures rose so high that men would sometimes faint from heat exhaustion.

And besides, the events of the courtroom the day before were still fresh in Meshach's mind. If anything else should happen at the royal palace, he wanted to be there to witness it.

"Did you sleep well last night?" Eli asked Meshach.

"I'll say I did." Meshach wiped the sweat from his forehead with the back of his hand. "After all that excitement yesterday, I slept like a baby."

"Well, you can be sure that there will be more excitement where that came from." Eli gave his son a knowing wink.

"I hope so," Meshach called over his shoulder as he turned to go to one of the storerooms to get some more grain for grinding. "Moses and Aaron sure have courage. More than I think I would have."

"He's got more courage than he knows what's good for him," snarled a voice behind Meshach. A shadow darkened the doorway of the storeroom. It was Seti, the Egyptian boy who also worked in the kitchen. He stood with his hands on his hips as if challenging Meshach to an argument or even a fight.

Meshach just stood looking at Seti, not knowing what to do. He should have guessed Seti would have something to say about the showdown in Pharaoh's court the day before.

"Just who do you Hebrews think you are?" Seti taunted. "Ha! Slaves! That's what you are! Moses, your so-called deliverer, has no business telling us Egyptians what the Hebrews will and will not do!" There was scorn in Seti's voice, and Meshach could see the muscles in his arms and neck tighten.

Meshach straightened up to make himself as tall as he could. "We may be slaves now, but someday we will be free." Meshach hoped that he didn't sound afraid. He wanted to be bold and brave, but right now he felt very small and unimportant. With shaking hands he scooped up a basketful of wheat from a pile of grain on the floor and then lifted the basket to his shoulder.

"Free!" Seti sneered. "You will always be slaves in Egypt, because Ra is all-powerful! He is the rising sun of Egypt, and Pharaoh is his son! All nations must bow to the will of Ra and Amenhotep." Seti spat on the floor. "Your God is weak, if He lives at all! Where is His image? I'd like to see it!"

Meshach swallowed hard. He had no image of Jehovah, but that was because Hebrews were not supposed to make images to Him. Meshach knew that from all the stories his father had told him about Abraham, Isaac, and Jacob.

But there were other reasons too. No one really knew what Jehovah looked like. Meshach remembered the story about Father Abraham entertaining Jehovah and the two angels. And then there was the story about Jacob wrestling with Jehovah the night before he met Esau. But what did Jehovah really look like? Did He have arms and legs like people, or did He just make Himself look like a human when He appeared to Abraham and Jacob?

Meshach didn't know what to say. He didn't want to fight Seti, but he was afraid it might come to that. He could tell it was what Seti wanted. Meshach wasn't sure he could be brave and stand up for Jehovah right now, but he knew how he'd feel if he didn't.

And then suddenly the pride in his Hebrew heritage welled up inside of Meshach—it didn't really matter what Jehovah looked like. Jehovah was Meshach's God. He was the God of the Hebrews. Meshach knew he had to do something.

Meshach stepped toward Seti. "My God is Jehovah!" he said, sticking his chin out proudly. "He is the One and Only Invisible God. I wish you could know Him as I do, Seti. Before many days pass, the whole world will know that He is Lord of heaven and earth, and that there is no God like Him." The words were coming easier now. "And Seti," Meshach added confidently, "Jehovah will set us free! He has promised it!"

Meshach stepped toward the doorway, and Seti moved to the side to let him pass. Meshach hoped he looked as brave as he felt. He could feel Seti glaring at him as he walked back into the kitchen. Meshach began pouring some grain into a large hollowed-out stone mortar. With a round stone he began to rub the grain back and forth. Over and over again he ground it, until flour had formed in the bottom of the mortar.

"Son, I'm proud of you," Eli's low voice spoke softly over Meshach's shoulder. Meshach turned and smiled.

"You heard our conversation?"

"It was hard not to—Seti was shouting." Eli smiled, and then added, "You did well. You kept things from getting out of hand, and yet you spoke up in the name of Jehovah." Eli laid a hand on Meshach's shoulder. "You stood for Jehovah just as we expect He will soon stand up for us."

Meshach grinned again. It felt good to know that he had stood up for something he believed in. Meshach scooped the flour out of the mortar and then put in some more wheat. He began grinding the grain again, until he had enough flour for another batch of bread.

The smell of warm bread filled the kitchen, reminding Meshach that the morning's first batch of bread must be finished baking. He straightened his back and went to help his father take the golden brown loaves from the ovens.

It was only midmorning, but already Meshach was hungry. He broke off a piece of bread and let the aroma fill his nostrils before he bit into it. It smelled delicious. The round flat bread was used by the Egyptians for nearly every meal; it was a main part of their diet.

As Meshach slid the wooden paddles under the crusty loaves, Hatsuret, the chief steward of the palace, entered the kitchen. "Eli," he called as he laid a piece of papyrus on one of the wooden tables, "I've got an important task for you. Pharaoh Amenhotep has summoned all the governors of the provinces to come to the royal palace for their yearly feast in honor of the gods Osiris and Isis. This is the time of year when everyone prays for the seasonal blessings of prosperity throughout the land, so it's important, as I'm sure you know."

He smiled and looked directly at Eli. "The governors have also brought their wives with them, and Queen Tiye is providing a banquet for them tonight. She has asked that you serve them personally. She speaks highly of your skills in the bakery here."

Eli wiped his face with a white linen cloth and then bowed from the waist. "Queen Tiye is too kind. However, I will be honored to do my best and see that she is not disappointed."

"Very well, then. Here is the list of banquet items she has requested. You will note that there are several specialty items—sesame cakes, honey wafers, and those fancy melon platters of yours. She says she knows of no one who makes them quite like you do." Hatsuret raised his eyebrows. "You are a splendid baker, Eli, and you know how to put on quite a show with your delicacies."

Hatsuret slid the parchment toward Eli.

"I will begin the preparations immediately," Eli bowed again. "What time does she wish to be served?"

"At dusk, just after the evening lamps have been lit. And now, I must be going," he added as he turned to leave. "I have much to do, myself, before then."

Eli immediately began making preparations for the feast. "Meshach," he called, "go to the storeroom and collect the ingredients we will need. Bring the fine flour from the large stone jar on the shelf and ask Seti for some of the honey they use to flavor the beer."

Meshach turned to obey his father, but he was afraid. He didn't want to talk to Seti—he didn't want another confrontation so soon after the first meeting in the storeroom.

However, he needn't have worried. Suddenly there was a shout in the corridor leading to the kitchens.

"We're cursed! We're cursed!" Saatet came running into the kitchen. His eyes were big and his breathing was heavy. "There's trouble at the Nile! A scourge has descended upon the river of life!"

The other Egyptian workers in the kitchen ran together at the center of the room, surrounding Saatet as he staggered in. Sweat trickled down his face and chest.

"What happened?" Eli demanded, setting down a basket of loaves.

"We are doomed, I tell you!" Saatet wailed, his eyes darting from one person in the group to the next. "They have cursed Egypt!"

CHAPTER 10

"Saatet!" Eli pushed his way to the front of the group. "Slow down! Stop babbling! Tell us what happened!"

Saatet took a deep breath and swallowed hard as though he were growing faint. Then his shoulders slumped, and he sank to his knees on the floor.

Meshach knew that Saatet was superstitious—most people in Egypt were. Saatet was afraid of unlucky numbers. He was afraid of any animal that was black, and he was especially afraid of being around anything that had died. Meshach felt sorry for him. Saatet didn't know Jehovah and the peace a person could have if he trusted in Jehovah. Whatever it was he had seen or heard had spooked him for sure.

"I was at the Nile," Saatet moaned. "I was with the royal family for their early morning purification rites. I go with Pharaoh Amenhotep and Queen Tiye every morning at dawn to bless the river and the god Osiris. When we arrived this morning, the chieftain, Moses, and his brother, Aaron, were there to meet us!"

Saatet took a quick breath and shook his head as if he were trying to get the memory of it all out of his mind. "I'll never forget the sight as long as I live," he groaned. "As soon as Aaron started talking, I had this terrible feeling that something bad was going to happen. I could feel it in my bones. I could tell by the tone of his voice." Saatet put his hands to his face.

"Aaron said that the God of the Hebrews had a special message for Pharaoh. He said that because of Amenhotep's stubbornness in refusing to let the slaves go worship Jehovah, calamity is about to come upon Egypt."

"Calamity?" Eli was persistent. "What kind of calamity?"

"The Nile!" Saatet croaked. "Aaron told everyone on the riverbank that he was going to strike the water of the Nile with his shepherd's rod and that the water in the Nile would change into blood! He said the fish would die, too, and that the river would soon begin to stink!"

"So, what happened then?" demanded one of the servants.

Saatet's eyes began to dart about wildly, and his breathing became more rapid.

Eli laid a hand on Saatet's shoulder to calm him down. "Go on," he urged.

Saatet took a deep breath. "Well, it happened just like Aaron said it would! He reached out with his rod and touched the water where it laps up against Pharaoh's steps that go down into the water." Saatet began to lose control of his voice as it rose in pitch. "It turned, I'm telling you! It did! The water began to turn into blood right before our very eyes."

"You saw this happen?" someone asked unbelievingly.

"It happened, I tell you! I was there! The water turned to blood! It was awful!" Saatet began to shake and then weep. "What are we going to do?" he wailed. "The Nile is the source of all life. How will we survive without its life-giving waters?"

Everyone stared at Saatet. A deathly silence fell over the room as each person realized the seriousness of the situation. Most of the servants in the room were Egyptians. Meshach knew that they worshiped the Nile as their god. In fact every god in Egypt was somehow tied to the worship of the Nile River—the Nile truly did bring life to Egypt.

In the spring at flood tide, the Nile always stretched way beyond its normal banks. When the waters went down, rich river mud was always left behind that made wonderful soil for growing crops. Would the polluted water of the river now ruin the land so that the crops wouldn't grow?

Worse still, now that the Nile River was polluted, how would everyone find enough water to drink? Most of Egypt was a desert. Any water that had already been drawn from the river would have to be rationed. More wells would have to be dug, but there was never a guarantee that new wells would provide water.

Suddenly a servant woman in the kitchen let out a scream. "It's true!" she shrieked. "The water has turned to blood!" and then she fainted dead away. As she toppled to the floor, a clay cup she was holding fell from her hand, spilling the contents on the floor. A red liquid spread across the floor like a pool of blood.

Saatet jumped to his feet, knocking over a large clay jar of water, and more of the same red liquid spread rapidly across the tiled kitchen floor.

In an instant, everyone was running about the room, scrambling to get away from the ever-widening stain on the floor. They rushed for the door, screaming as though their last day on earth had come. Everyone, that is, except Meshach and his father.

As the room emptied, Eli and Meshach simply stood watching the blood-red liquid.

"The judgments promised by Jehovah have begun." Eli bowed his head solemnly. "They reach even to the water we drink and the cups we hold in our hands."

Meshach thought for a moment. "How is that possible, Father? Moses cursed the Nile, but the water we drink here in the kitchen was drawn last night."

"It's a miracle, Son. A strange and miraculous scourge upon the land."

Meshach bowed his head. "Then, it has finally begun just as Moses said it would. Do you think this is the beginning of the end?" He said the words softly. "Do you think that our deliverance is at hand?"

Eli looked out the open doorway to the River Nile beyond. "I believe it is, my son."

"Then I want to go to the Nile and see this great wonder for myself."

The two of them trudged the distance to the river and stood on the bank staring at the scene before them. "The half was not told us," Eli murmured. "Just look at that sea of red."

"The whole river has turned to blood," Meshach whispered, stunned at the fearful sight before them. "All of it."

"This is indeed the hand of God, and He knows just how to hit the Egyptians where it hurts the most."

"You mean because of Osiris, the god of the Nile?"

"Partly." Eli glanced at Meshach. "But it's more than that, I'd say. You see, the Nile is a very symbolic part of Egypt's way of life. Think about it. The Nile is the life blood of Egypt, and now God has turned the river itself into blood."

Eli and Meshach returned to the kitchen, but there was not much they could do. They couldn't bake anything that required water. All the cisterns and clay jars of water were full of the polluted liquid that looked and even smelled like blood.

In the palace and on the palace grounds there was much commotion. No one really knew what anyone else was doing. Meshach and Eli wished they could help somehow, but they finally just gave up and went home.

When they arrived at home, however, things were not much better. People were running here and there pouring out the contents of cups, pitchers, and water jars. The same blood-red liquid was in the homes of the Hebrews. Meshach could hardly believe his eyes as his mother, Jerusha, met them at the door.

"What's the meaning of this plague that has overrun Egypt?" she asked fearfully.

"It's the hand of Jehovah." Eli's voice was steady. "Jehovah is beginning to stand up for His people."

"Stand up for His people!" Meshach could hear his mother's voice tremble. "You call this standing up for His people! The land is filled with blood! There's nothing to drink!"

Meshach stood looking at his mother. It was true. Evil had come to the homes of the Hebrew slaves too. Were the Hebrew slaves no different in God's eyes from the Egyptians? Was the God of Abraham, Isaac, and Jacob weak, as Seti had said He was? Would He truly stand up for His people?

CHAPTER 11

By the next morning the stench from the river was beginning to fill the land, and pure water was impossible to find. The river was clogged with the thick red ooze, and all the streams that flowed into the Nile had become like blood. Even the ponds, small lakes, and backwaters from the overflow of the flooded Nile had turned a stagnant red.

Meshach stood with his father overlooking the Nile once again as the sun's orange circle rose over the eastern horizon. Dead fish had begun washing up on the bank at the river's edge, and now and then a dead goat or cow floated by. Already flies were gathering for a feast of rotting flesh. Meshach held his nose. The odor was almost overpowering, and it had barely been twenty-four hours since the water had turned. It made Meshach's stomach sick just to look at any of it.

"What will we do for water?" Meshach finally asked his father.

Eli looked at Meshach, concern written on his face. "We'll have to dig wells like everyone else is doing," he replied.

Meshach frowned and shook his head. "But Father, that's a lot of work, and we don't even know if we'll find water."

"There's not much else we can do, Son."

And so they dug, and as Meshach had guessed, it wasn't easy. Several families got together to help dig for the water they hoped to share. At first the work went quickly because the ground near the surface was sandy, but below the first layers of sand, the ground was more like clay and full of gravel. It was so hard that they had to use a mattock so that they could chop away at the hard soil. And to haul the soil up to the surface, they had to use baskets.

Meshach worked with his father and Uncle Heber for several hours that first morning. Eli's older cousins Nadab and Abihu helped too. They all wanted to make some headway before the hottest hours of the day set in, but the going was slow. By noon the well shafts were still not very deep.

"There's not much more we can do now," Eli said as he leaned on the wall of the deepening hole and wiped the sweat from his brow with the back of his arm. "If we keep going like this, we're going to die of heat stroke. We need the water, but it won't help us if we die out here in the sun trying to get it."

"You're right!" Uncle Heber panted. "We'll just have to come out and start again after the heat of the day has passed."

"That's fine by me," Eli agreed. "Nadab? Abihu? Can you come out and help again too?"

Nadab went to the shade of a date palm tree and sat down. "All right, I suppose that's the only thing we can do," he agreed, "but I've got two small children at home, so we need to get some water soon."

He looked at Eli. "I, for one, would like to know where the God of Abraham is at a time like this! If you ask me, I think He's abandoned us! This whole thing is a dreadful disaster!" Nadab's forehead wrinkled into a frown, and Meshach could tell that he was more than just afraid. He was angry. "I thought that Moses said the Lord was going to do marvelous things for His people! Well, where is He now? Where are the marvelous signs that Moses promised us?"

Meshach stared at Nadab. How could he say such things! How could he speak against Jehovah, the Great I AM! Jehovah was everywhere! Surely Nadab knew that Jehovah could hear the horrible things he was saying!

Eli sat down in the shade beside Nadab. "We are seeing the signs Jehovah promised us. The plague of blood is a sign," he replied. "This is just the beginning of what Jehovah will do to make Pharaoh see that He must let us go."

"These are the signs?" Nadab retorted. "Well, if that's the case, how is it that Pharaoh's magicians can also turn water into blood?"

"This has happened?" Several of the men sitting nearby turned to listen to the conversation. Meshach could see fear in their eyes.

"I heard it just this morning!" Nadab glanced around the group of men, a look of triumph on his face.

Eli's face grew stern. "Their power to do such things does not come from God, but from the evil one." He shook his head. "Moses, on the other hand, uses the power of Jehovah to perform such signs."

"How do we know that?" Nadab blurted.

"Because we know that no man has the power to do such things. Think about it!" Eli insisted. "Only the powers of the spirit world can work miracles. Men can do such things only through the power of Jehovah or through the magic incantations of the evil one." Eli paused, and then his voice grew strong with conviction as he turned to look at all the men sitting in the shade.

"I'm telling you, brothers—be patient! Wait and see what the Lord our God will do! Don't be afraid! Jehovah is all-powerful, and He will stand up for His people!"

"Well, if He is all-powerful," Nadab kept on, "why has He brought this terrible plague on the Hebrews too? Why not just the Egyptians? They're the pagans in the land!"

No one said anything more. It was obvious to Meshach that no matter what his father said, Nadab would only argue. It seemed that Nadab just wanted to find reasons to fuss and whine and grumble against Moses and Jehovah.

Meshach sat thinking about the conversation between the two men. *Why did God allow the plague to come upon everyone? Why not just the Egyptians, as Nadab has argued? Is it somehow a test of our faith?*

All during the heat of the day the men sat in the shade of their small mud-brick homes, trying to save their energy and body moisture for the job ahead. By late afternoon word came from the royal city of Tanis that many Egyptians had collapsed in the hot sun, trying to dig wells too.

The sun was low in the sky when the men began their work again. Meshach and his cousins, Asher and Zicri, helped too, but they got tired more quickly than the men did. Even the women came to help pull the baskets of sand, gravel, and clay to the surface and empty them. And they all took turns holding the sooty torches so that the workers could see in the darkness.

At midnight a shout went up that water was beginning to seep into the shaft they had dug. And it was pure. There was not even the slightest tinge of red in the water. However, it was only a small trickle, and even though they dug down several cubits deeper, only a small pool of water was collecting at the bottom of the hole. Thirsty hands reached for cups of the cool water and gulped it down.

Eli stood to his feet and tried to straighten his aching back. "Well, men, it's obvious that the hole we've dug is not going to provide enough water for all our families."

There were worried looks on all the men's faces.

"Then what are we going to do?" Nadab demanded. "We worked this morning, and now much of the night. If we don't get enough water, our families will wither like the fields during a drought!"

"We'll just have to dig again—in another place, of course."

"Another place! Again! What good will that do?" Nadab held a torch above his head so he could see Eli's face. "If this is all the water we get each time, we'll have to dig a score of holes to get enough water. There are over forty people in our combined families, and plenty more people will come begging for water once they discover we have some." He scowled at Eli in the light of the torch.

And Nadab was right, or so it appeared to Meshach. Already footsteps could be heard coming from every direction as people heard the good news that water had been found. When a crowd of onlookers pushed their way to the edge of the well, Nadab swung his torch around to keep them from coming any closer.

CHAPTER 12

"Stand back!" Nadab shouted. "Stand back, I tell you! Don't come any closer! This well belongs to the families of the house of Uzziel. There is none for you!" He glared at them all menacingly and held the torch out in front of him as if it were some kind of sword. "Go on about your business and find your own water!"

Eli stepped forward and raised his voice. "Now, just a minute! You can't treat people like this! These people are your brothers! They are the flesh and blood of Israel!"

Nadab turned the torch on Eli. "They can get their own water! This is ours!" His face looked so angry and his voice sounded so determined that Eli finally backed off.

Nadab then turned to look at the other family members standing around. His eyes squinted in the light of the torch, and Meshach could see his teeth clenched together. "If any of you want to dig another well, go right ahead, but I'm going to stand guard over the water we already have in this well! I'm not going to let anyone else profit from the hard work we've already done!"

All that night the rest of the men and boys dug. More family members came to help with the digging, and by morning light the family had dug two more wells. They had chosen a spot near a small stream, and each of these new wells produced more water than the first one had.

As day dawned, Meshach could see hundreds of wells being dug all up and down the Nile River valley.

In the afternoon, a detachment of Egyptian soldiers from the city came into the settlement at Goshen and ordered several hundred men to go with them. Eli was one of the men taken. When Eli didn't come back for several days, Meshach guessed that Pharaoh must have heard about the success the Hebrews were having in digging wells. He would need slave labor to help dig his own wells.

The smell from the Nile hadn't gotten any better by the end of the week, but everyone had gotten used to it by now. The little bit of water they managed to get from their wells was enough to drink, but that was about all. Very little cooking could be done, and of course no one could take a bath. Meshach was almost glad for it. He hated taking baths, anyway, except to cool off. Before the plague of blood, he had always liked jumping into the Nile for a swim with his cousins, but now that was impossible. Meshach had tried putting his hand in the water of the Nile once, but the feel of the blood-red water on his skin made him tingle.

There was no end in sight for the plague of blood, and everyone was beginning to get anxious. Would the Nile eventually become clear again, or would it always be red? Worse still, would anyone get sick from the disease that was sure to follow? Would anyone die?

By now Meshach's father was back, tired, but none the worse for his days of digging wells. However, things were not going so well for Moses and Aaron.

Eli came home one night talking about Moses and Aaron meeting with the tribal elders. There had been a lot of arguing among the leaders. Many criticized Moses, and some even questioned God's leading. Meshach couldn't believe his ears as he listened to his father tell about the meeting. Apparently, Korah, one of Moses and Aaron's distant cousins, had been the most outspoken member of the tribal council.

"If this is Jehovah's way of punishing Pharaoh and all Egypt, then let it be so," Korah had complained, "but leave us out of it! Why must we suffer too? It's Pharaoh's lesson to learn, not ours!"

"That's right!" several others shouted.

"Now just a minute!" Moses had interrupted. "Jehovah knows what He's doing! Be strong and courageous, Brothers! Don't let this plague cause your faith in Jehovah to waver. It's a test of character for us all!"

"A test of character!" Korah jeered. "Why do we need a test of character? Haven't all these years of slavery tested our characters enough?" He paused and looked around the room. "We don't need character! What we need is deliverance from Egypt and Pharaoh Amenhotep!"

"And we will have it!" Moses shot right back. "We will! We—just—need to give Jehovah time to work things out in His own way and in His own good time!"

Korah stood up, his face turning a deep red as he looked straight at Moses. "In His own good time! Well, I say now's as good a time as any." He clenched his fist, waving it in the air. "Who died and set you up as our leader, anyway? Look at all the trouble you've caused us! It's been a week now, and Pharaoh still hasn't given in! He's increased our work load now so that we have to gather all the straw to make his bricks, and we still have to make the same number of bricks besides!"

Moses stood his ground. "Everything's going to be all right!" he insisted. "Jehovah said that with a mighty hand He would bring us out from under the Egyptians, and I believe Him. He promised to give us our inheritance in the land of milk and honey! What more can we ask for?"

"Milk and honey! Huh!" Korah spat the words out. "I'll believe it when I see it!"

Moses' face grew stern, and there was a long moment of silence as he glared at his cousin. "I'm ashamed of you, Korah! How dare you question Jehovah! How dare you mock His name and His holy purpose for our nation! You, of all people, ought to be able to stand bravely for Him!"

Moses turned to look over the entire group of elders. "And I'm ashamed of you all, too!" he added. "Hear this! You will see Jehovah's mighty hand as He strikes Egypt with many more plagues—plagues far worse than this plague of blood! You will see Israel delivered from bondage, my brothers, and taste the sweetness of freedom, but because of your hard hearts, you will not live to see Canaan!"

Silence hung over the group. Was Moses a prophet? Only prophets could make such predictions. Could he see the future, or were his words really Jehovah's words?

Moses stood tall and straight as he raised his shepherd's rod in his outstretched hand. "Tomorrow I am going to Pharaoh once again to ask that he let Israel go. I know that he will not let Israel go—not yet, but I must obey the command of Jehovah anyway. I have no other choice!"

Meshach stared at his father, the story finished. "You say this all happened tonight, here in Goshen!" Meshach's eyes were wide with excitement.

"It did, Son, and tomorrow there will be another showdown between Moses and Pharaoh."

"A showdown?" Meshach asked. "That could mean more trouble for all of us, couldn't it?"

"It could, Son, but one thing's for sure—as Jehovah promised our father Jacob so many years ago, He will watch over our people wherever we go. He will bring us back to the land of Canaan."

CHAPTER 13

By the time Meshach awoke the next morning, the Hebrew settlements at Goshen were already buzzing with a message from Moses. Another plague was on its way. Frogs.

"Frogs!" Meshach heard his mother shudder. "Not another plague! The plague of blood isn't even over yet!

"I hate frogs!" She made a face at Meshach's big sister, Kezia. "They're slippery, and they stink! As long as they stay in the river and ponds, they're fine, but keep them out of my house!" She looked worried, but said no more.

So a plague of frogs was coming! Meshach smiled as he thought about the little creatures. How could a little frog harm anyone? Of course for anyone who hated frogs as much as his mother did, the frogs would be a nuisance, maybe, but a plague?

Meshach could hardly imagine what a plague of frogs would be like. He had never even thought of such a thing. *Will giant frogs come hopping out of the river? Will they be poisonous, and will they bite people?* If the plague of blood hadn't been so serious, Meshach might have laughed at the idea of giant frogs, but he didn't.

Evidently Pharaoh had refused to listen to Moses. That was the story being given by the messenger who now stood in the narrow streets and lanes of Goshen. Evidently, Pharaoh Amenhotep didn't seem to care that the waters of Egypt were still polluted with the dark stain of blood. He knew that Moses had called upon Jehovah to bring the plague of blood in the first place, and he knew Moses was the only one who could take it away. Pharaoh's own magicians certainly couldn't.

Even worse, Amenhotep hadn't been able to bathe or worship at the riverside for over a week now. That would mean his god, Osiris, lord of the Nile, was somehow weaker than Jehovah.

"If you think that turning the Nile red is going to get me to release hundreds of thousands of slaves, then you have another think coming!" he had told Moses sternly.

It was amazing how fast news could travel in Egypt!

In spite of the seriousness of the message, Meshach grinned as he listened to the messenger tell the tale out in the street. If this was some kind of a standoff between Pharaoh and Moses, it was going to be a long, painful one. The ruler of the greatest nation on earth was opposing the great God of the universe, and obviously he had no idea whom he was dealing with.

Meshach did laugh to himself now, as he thought about it. Pharaoh Amenhotep and Jehovah? Ha! There was no contest!

And now the plague of frogs was on its way. No one knew when it would come or whether it would reach the land of Goshen. Would God protect the Hebrews from the likes of frogs? It hardly seemed necessary, Meshach thought.

Meshach went to eat his breakfast of bread and leban. As he squatted on the ground just outside the door of their home, he was told that his father had been summoned to the royal kitchens to work again. Water supplies were still scarce, and the Nile had not returned to normal, but Pharaoh and his household still needed to eat.

Meshach hoped that he would be able to go work at the kitchens with his father, but Jerusha surprised him with the announcement that she had time to help him practice his writing and reading skills. "Go get Asher," she commanded. "We might as well use our time wisely."

All that morning Meshach and Asher worked at copying the strange characters Jerusha wrote for them on a bare whitewashed wall inside their home. Even inside the house the air was uncomfortably warm as they used special sticks to press the letters of the Hebrew language into moist clay tablets.

While the boys practiced, Jerusha busied herself with tasks around the house. There was always something to do. She and Kezia worked at pounding grain in a mortar so that they could make a little bread. Without much water, they could make enough bread to last only a day or two. And of course there were always the goats to milk and sewing that needed to be done. By late afternoon, Jerusha needed to tend to another pregnant woman who lived several houses down and across the narrow alley. This was good news to Meshach—he was now free to go play.

He grabbed his cousins, Asher and Zicri, and ran for the river. It had been a few days since they had seen the Nile, and they were anxious to see what it looked like now. The water smelled worse than ever, and rotting fish lay dead along its banks. Maggots crawled all over the fish, and ravens and vultures were there by the hundreds, picking apart the scales and fins that were left.

Meshach and his cousins held their noses. All around them on the ground, frogs sat croaking. They must have left the river to escape the stinking water now turned almost black. Meshach wasn't surprised. If he were a frog, he wouldn't want to live in the river either, the way it looked and smelled now.

On the way back to the house, along the pathway Meshach saw a large frog almost as big around as his wrist. As he reached down to pick it up, it didn't even try to hop away. "I'm taking this one home." Meshach grinned at Asher and Zicri. "Maybe I can scare Kezia with it."

But when he reached home, he realized he would have to hide the frog if he didn't want his mother to find it. He grabbed a small clay pot sitting inside the door, put the frog in it, and then quickly laid a cover on the pot. He poked his head in the doorway to see if his mother was around but didn't see her anywhere.

Suddenly Meshach heard his mother's voice coming up the narrow street. "I'm sorry I'm home so late, Meshach," she called to him where he stood in the open doorway. "Could you stir the coals for the evening meal? Your father will be home soon, and we haven't even got anything prepared for the evening meal."

Meshach ran to a corner of the room and hid the pot behind a basket. He'd have to find a way to move the pot later when his mother wasn't looking.

At the evening meal, Meshach listened to news from the palace. Talk of the next plague was everywhere, but the idea of frogs being a problem didn't seem nearly as terrible as the plague of blood. How could it be? Frogs were harmless. They were pets that little boys carried around with them. The thought that green croakers could ever become a problem in Egypt was the last thing anyone was worrying about right now.

"Amenhotep laughed when Moses and Aaron told him that the next scourge on the land would be swarms of frogs," Eli said with a twitch of a smile on his face. "Frogs!" Eli imitated the Pharaoh's voice perfectly as he puckered up his forehead and tried to sound stern. "We're supposed to be afraid of frogs? Moses! You're going to have to do better than that! If this is the best your God can do, then you Hebrews are going to be in Egypt for a very long time!"

Meshach laughed at his father's imitation of the Pharaoh, but the thought of being stuck in Egypt forever didn't sound so funny.

He wished he could have been in the palace to hear the conversations between Pharaoh Amenhotep and Moses and all the advisors. That would have been something! Great men of Egypt in Pharaoh's court talking about little green frogs. Meshach fell asleep chuckling to himself over the very idea of it! No wonder Pharaoh had laughed.

Sometime in the night, Meshach dreamed of frogs. There were thousands of them everywhere! It was great! You could reach down and scoop them up by the armfuls, but you had to be careful that you didn't step on them because they covered the ground.

And then Meshach woke up. The moon was now low in the western sky, and the rooftop where he slept had an eerie glow about it. Meshach turned over on his reed mat. He wasn't sure what had awakened him, but at first he thought he must be camping out down by the river because he could hear frogs croaking. Lots of them.

Suddenly he remembered about the frog he had put in the clay pot. He had forgotten to move the pot or take the frog out. He hoped the frog wasn't dead. Frogs could dry out pretty quickly away from water. He had meant to put water in the pot before he went to sleep, but it was probably too late now.

Meshach tried to go back to sleep, but something wasn't right. What it was he couldn't quite say, but one thing was sure—those croaking frogs were almost deafening. How could they be making so much noise clear up in Goshen, away from the river?

Meshach sat up and crawled over to the edge of the rooftop. As his eyes adjusted to the darkened street below, he thought he could see the ground moving. And the croaking of frogs was now almost roaring in his ears. He tried to clear the fog from his sleepy mind. What was going on?

And then suddenly Meshach was wide awake as it dawned on him what was happening. The plague of frogs was happening! It had to be! Meshach could see that the ground was literally covered with hopping, croaking frogs! Thousands of them!

CHAPTER 14

Could it possibly be? Was it actually happening? Had Moses' words come true as he said they would?

Meshach had laughed when he first heard that a plague of frogs was coming. Of course he knew that Jehovah had the power to do whatever He said He would do, but to have it actually happen was quite another thing!

Meshach wasn't used to so many things happening in such a short time. First, he had seen Aaron's rod eat up all the other rods—or rather serpents—of Pharaoh's priest magicians. Then he and Seti had almost gotten into a fight. Then the plague of blood had come to stink up the land, and now an army of frogs had arrived. It was too much!

The peace and quiet of the night was gone as thousands of frogs sat croaking in the street below. Meshach had almost forgotten that there was a house full of people down below him, and a street full of homes just like his, and settlements with thousands of Hebrew families like theirs.

And then, almost as if by magic, everyone in the house below suddenly awakened and began screaming—Mother, Kezia, and Chilion—and Father was shouting. Meshach could hear them running around in the house knocking over clay jars—and then he could see them running out into the street, only to find that they were stepping on thousands of slimy, croaking, jumping frogs. But then there was nothing for them to do but run back into the house to get away from the nightmare of frogs.

If it hadn't been so scary for Meshach himself to see everyone going crazy with fright, he might have laughed out loud at how silly the whole thing looked.

And then every house in Goshen was awake at the same moment, it seemed! People were running everywhere! And because everyone was still half asleep, the whole thing seemed even worse. Meshach knew just what they must be thinking! What on earth were these squirming creatures doing crawling around under their feet as everyone raced up and down the narrow streets of Goshen? People lost their balance as they slipped on the slimy street covering of frogs, and then scrambled to their feet again only to bump into someone else doing the very same thing! This, of course, made them slip and fall once again among the wriggling swarm of croaking, jumping frogs.

By morning light it was obvious that this was the worst invasion of frogs the land had ever seen. Even the oldest folks in Goshen said they couldn't remember ever seeing so many frogs! Meshach's cousin Zicri said his great-grandfather had seen a bad plague of frogs when he was just a boy, but it was nothing like this one.

The next few days were an ordeal for everyone. The frogs were pests because they were everywhere. Meshach couldn't go anywhere without seeing the frogs. They were in the streets; they were in the marketplaces where the Hebrews sold the few vegetables they managed to grow in their small gardens. They jumped into the wells that the Hebrews had so painstakingly dug. They even got into the storehouses where Pharaoh kept the government grain.

Worse still, they were in everyone's homes. Meshach's family couldn't escape the little green animals. They hopped into water jars, into the open pots where food was kept, and into the baskets of lentils or chickpeas. They sat croaking in the bread troughs where the bread dough was kneaded, and they jumped into the little clay ovens even while the fires were going. The smell of their flesh was sickening as they scorched and then turned black in the flames.

Meshach couldn't remember how many times he had heard his mother and sister scream out in surprise and anger as the frogs continually pestered the family. No one could sit down to eat anymore—now they had to stand while eating. It was beginning to wear everyone down.

But the worst of it all was the nuisance the frogs made of themselves at nighttime. No one could sleep because the frogs made so much noise croaking, and the slimy things were continually hopping over their beds or into them. Each night Meshach had to shake out his goat-hair blanket to make a place for himself to sleep. And each morning he had to shake out his clothes to get rid of the ten or twelve frogs that had hidden there during the night.

And every neighbor had the same problem. It wasn't uncommon to hear people shouting in frustration as they would find frogs in even more unexpected places.

It became a trial for everyone, but especially for Moses. The Hebrew elders weren't blaming Moses for the plague of frogs, but they were blaming him for Pharaoh's new attitude. Neither the plague of blood or the plague of frogs had made Pharaoh change his mind. He still hadn't budged on his promise to keep the slaves in Egypt. And he was making them work harder than ever before!

"You'll continue to make mud bricks for Pharaoh's building projects!" the slave overseers had shouted at the Hebrew foremen. "You've got too much time on your hands if you are thinking of freedom!"

Not surprisingly, the foremen had come to the elders, frustrated and angry. "How can we make bricks?" they protested. "Pharaoh no longer provides the straw we need to mix in with the mud to make the bricks! And besides," they complained, "we have so many other problems in the settlement, now, with the plague of blood and frogs! Our wives are going crazy!"

And the Egyptians were having their own set of problems. Since the Egyptians worshiped frogs, the plague of frogs had become their worst nightmare. Eli explained it over supper one evening.

"Heqa, the Egyptian frog-headed goddess, has been worshiped for as long as anyone can remember. She's one of the Nile goddesses, and now with the frogs everywhere, that creates a big problem for all the priests."

Eli glanced around the small room as he ate his bowl of pottage. Again the family was having to stand while they ate—it was the only way to keep the frogs out of the food they were eating. Eli broke a round, flat loaf of bread in two and handed one piece to Meshach.

"I think I've seen statues of Haqa." Meshach scowled as he glanced down at the floor where frogs hopped over and around his feet. "And you mean to tell me that they worship these things?" he said as he kicked several of the frogs away from his bare feet. "How can the Egyptians think that these dumb little frogs can do anything for them? They're nothing but a nuisance!"

"You're right!" Eli chuckled. "There's nothing wonderful about a frog hopping into your bowl of pottage. Lentils and onions taste good together, but a frog thrown in the pot for good measure is going a bit too far!"

Meshach loved his father's sense of humor. They both laughed as they took bites of the lentil pottage from the clay bowls they held in their hands. For a few moments it was good to laugh again. Everyone had been so angry and frustrated since the plague of blood had begun, and now with the thousands of frogs climbing over and into everything, Meshach had almost forgotten what it was like to laugh.

"But wait!" Eli continued with a chuckle. "There's more! These Egyptians are comedians! Everybody in Egypt is laughing now at the latest news to come out of the palace. After the frogs began to swarm into the cities, Pharaoh Amenhotep was so anxious to prove that his gods were stronger than Jehovah—or at least, as strong. Anyway, so he ordered his priests to use their magic to try and make more frogs like the ones Jehovah has sent."

"More frogs?" Meshach couldn't believe his ears.

"That's right." Eli grinned. "And that's exactly what Pharaoh's advisors were saying when they heard he was asking such a thing. 'Wait a minute!' they said. 'Egypt already has too many frogs, and you're asking your priests to make more?' "

And then Meshach really did laugh! He laughed so hard that tears came to his eyes!

"And now for the really good news," Eli announced, when the laughter had finally died down. "I've heard that Pharaoh has finally called for Moses and Aaron to come and talk about a truce. The frogs have finally gotten to him and the royal family, to say nothing of the priests."

"Then you think Pharaoh will change his mind about letting us go?" Meshach asked. He looked at his father excitedly as he ate the last bites of his bread. "If the frogs over at the palace are even half as bad as they are here, then Pharaoh's advisors and priests must be going crazy!"

"Oh, they're going crazy, all right!" Eli frowned as he stood to his feet and made his way toward the doorway of the house, stepping over frogs as he went. "The frogs are far worse at the palace than they are here, if that can possibly be!"

"Worse?" Meshach followed his father out into the gathering darkness. "I'd love to see that!"

"They're worse—believe me!" Eli winked at Meshach. "One batch of bread I took out of the ovens this morning had frogs piled up all around the loaves—the frogs were charred to a crisp." Eli shook his head at the thought of it. "I didn't remember seeing that many hop into the oven when I slid the bread in."

Eli grew more serious. "But frogs or no frogs, it doesn't matter. Pharaoh Amenhotep is determined to keep us here in Egypt to work for him! I'm sure the plague will end eventually," Eli predicted. "Once the frogs are gone, though, Pharaoh will change his mind again and tell us we can't go."

Meshach frowned again, and his eyes narrowed to little slits. "Father, if Pharaoh Amenhotep can't see Jehovah's hand in these plagues, then he must really be a fool."

"A fool? Well, now, I can't argue with you there."

"He is. I mean, the frogs make us frustrated, but they are more a bother than anything else. But, Father, if more judgments come, like you said before, then they will probably be worse than this one."

Eli laid his hand on Meshach's shoulder. "You are wise beyond your years, Son, and probably more right than you can possibly know. I just wish Pharaoh would see it that way."

CHAPTER 15

For the first time in several days, Meshach slept well. When he awoke in the grayness of early dawn, he felt fully rested. The sun was not quite up yet, but now something had awakened him. He couldn't quite decide what it was. Was it the early morning air—was it the smell of the morning meal being made in every home up and down the streets of Goshen? Was it the chatter of women bringing water in from the newly dug wells?

Meshach turned over on his reed mat. Suddenly he knew what it was. Everywhere in Goshen it was strangely silent. Deathly silent. No frogs could be heard croaking, or peeping, or chirping. Not one. Meshach had gotten so used to the droning sound of croaking frogs that he had almost forgotten what silence was like. And now the silence was wonderfully beautiful to his ears.

But what had happened to the frogs? Where had they gone? Had they all left town? Had they hopped back to the Nile River?

That was another thought. Was the river back to normal again?

Meshach jumped to his feet—there were too many questions waiting to be answered. He turned to his family, who had also begun sleeping on the roof with him—everyone was there, sprawled out on their reed sleeping mats—father, mother, Chilion, Kezia. It had become just too difficult to keep the frogs out of the house anymore, so sleeping on the roof seemed the only thing to do. A few of the frogs still managed to get up the narrow steps leading to the roof of the house, but there weren't as many.

Meshach looked at the sleeping forms of his family. Why hadn't they awakened yet? Mother and Father were always up before everyone else in the family. Maybe they had slept well, too, because of the quietness that had finally come to Goshen.

And the frogs?

Meshach looked out across the rooftops of the houses stretching to the east. He looked to the west, and then to the north in the direction of the Great Sea. Finally he looked over the edge of the roof to the street below, and the sight that met his eyes took him totally by surprise.

The frogs were dead! Hundreds of thousands of them littered the streets of Goshen! They were everywhere, and already on the early morning air he could smell their dead bodies.

Meshach had told his father that having frogs around wasn't the worst thing that could happen, but the picture of their dead bodies in the early morning light now changed his mind.

"The frogs are dead!" Meshach suddenly found his voice, shouting out the words as he raced down the narrow brick stairs along the outside wall of the house. He tried to avoid stepping on dead frogs as he ran, but there were just too many. Their soft, limp bodies made him almost slip several times.

And then almost as quickly, Meshach turned and raced back up the steps to the roof, realizing that his family still hadn't caught on to the wonderful news.

"The frogs are dead!" he shouted again. His mother had awakened by now and was sitting up. She took one look at Meshach's face and jumped to her feet as quickly as the early morning hour would allow.

"What's wrong, Son?"

"Mother!" he shouted excitedly. "Didn't you hear me? The frogs are dead! They're lying everywhere! Thousands and thousands of them!"

"The frogs are dead! All of them?" She rubbed her sleepy eyes. "How can that be?"

"Father! Wake up! The frogs are dead!" Meshach shouted, not answering her question.

Eli sat up on his mat, too, and sniffed the morning air. "They don't smell gone to me."

"Well, they're dead anyway, and now they won't bother us anymore."

"That's what you think," Eli retorted, as he got to his feet and went to look out over the edge of the flat rooftop. "We can thank the Lord that they are gone, but our troubles have only begun." He took one look at the frogs littering the street, and shook his head. "The worst part of the plague is upon us now."

Chilion and Kezia jumped up suddenly and hurried over to the edge of the roof.

Kezia shrieked at the sight below. "Oh! They're disgusting, and they smell awful!"

The entire family stood and stared at the frog-strewn street in the gathering light of dawn. Finally Meshach turned to his father. "When you said the worst part of the plague is upon us, Father, what did you mean?"

"Well, when they were alive, Meshach, the frogs were trouble, but now that they are dead, disease and sickness will spread throughout the land." Eli put his hands to his head. "How are we ever going to get rid of all these frogs?"

The day hadn't even started, and already Meshach's father looked tired.

"We can bury them," Meshach quickly replied. "That's what we usually do with dead animals."

"There are too many of them." Eli scratched his beard.

Jerusha began to weep softly. "Jehovah has abandoned us. Where is He when we need Him most?"

"Jehovah hasn't abandoned us," Eli said kindly but firmly as he put his arm around Jerusha's shoulder. "He hasn't allowed harm to come to us yet, and He won't fail us now."

Meshach looked at Kezia and Chilion. He knew his mother's faith in Jehovah was weak right now, and he was worried that her lack of faith might spread to them.

"Why don't we burn the frogs?" Meshach offered, trying to think up a quick solution. "There are so many of them, but we can burn them right in the streets."

"That's a great idea, Son." Eli laid a hand on Meshach's shoulder and turned to Jerusha. "Our son is no longer a boy. He's speaking more and more like a man every day!"

They said their morning prayers, dressed for the day, and quickly ate a few mouthfuls of bread. By now they could hear their neighbors out in the street. Exclamations of both fear and relief could be heard everywhere, and many were already holding their noses.

Father had been right. As the sun rose in all its strength, the smell was overwhelming, and already the flies were beginning to gather.

"Come on, everyone," Father called as he and Meshach began raking and sweeping the frogs into piles. "We've got to get some fires going before the flies arrive in real numbers!"

It was hard work, but by noon every frog on the street had been thrown on a pile and was smoldering. But now the stench of burning flesh was almost unbearable. Father found some chunks of pitch and threw them on the piles nearest their house so that the fires would burn hotter and more quickly.

"Do you think Pharaoh Amenhotep will let us go, now, Father?" Meshach wiped the sweat from his face with the sleeve of his tunic.

Eli shrugged. "Maybe, but I doubt it. Pharaoh is not known for his generosity, you know."

"Yes, but with the smell of all the dead frogs everywhere, I would think that he would have gotten the message." Meshach held his nose. "I know I have. Jehovah has control over all things—even the frogs. He can give them life, He can bring them in by the thousands, and He can kill them."

"Good point, Son, but Pharaoh is not a worshiper of Jehovah, and he is a very stubborn man. Once he sees that the frogs are dead and can be burned, he'll forget all about them—and his promise to let us go."

In the afternoon, soldiers arrived from the palace. Hundreds of Hebrew men were rounded up and herded off to the city, and Eli had to go with them. None of the men had gone to work that morning because of all the dead frogs, but now it was off to work again. If there were dead frogs to burn in Goshen, then there were probably even more up in Pharaoh's palace and the royal city of Tanis. Once again it was obvious that Amenhotep wanted the slaves to do for him what they had done so well for themselves.

No one enjoyed the meal that evening because of the smell that seemed to fill the entire land of Goshen. No matter where Meshach went, he couldn't get away from the stench of dead frogs and the horrible odor that their burning bodies made. Kezia and his mother didn't eat anything at all.

After the meal, Meshach decided to go over to Asher's house. When he arrived, Aaron was there talking to Asher's grandfather in the doorway to the house. Meshach caught snatches of what they were saying as the two boys played a game of stones in the street.

"Pharaoh Amenhotep has changed his mind," Aaron said dejectedly. "He's not going to let us go."

"Well, you didn't think it was going to be that easy, did you?" Asher's grandfather was busy making a basket out of woven reeds.

"No, but I was hoping something would happen to move us in the right direction," Aaron admitted. He squinted as he gazed at the slanting rays of the late afternoon sun. "A simple No from Amenhotep is hard to take. Now we're right back where we were before the plague of blood."

"So, what will happen next?"

"Another plague will come." Aaron shook his head sadly. "Moses and I will be going to court tomorrow morning to warn Pharaoh again, but it won't do any good. The way things are going, Pharaoh will turn us down again."

"How do you know that for sure?"

"Because Moses has said it will be so."

Meshach's heart began to beat faster. When he thought about another plague coming, he felt excited in a strange sort of way. Not because of the bad things that would happen, but because things were finally beginning to change in Egypt. The Hebrews had been waiting for deliverance from slavery for as long as anyone could remember—clear back to whenever—and now it looked like it might happen. Maybe really soon.

CHAPTER 16

Meshach wanted to ask Aaron all kinds of questions, and yet he was tongue-tied as he stared at this great man. He wanted to ask Aaron why Pharaoh was being so stubborn. He wanted to ask about the plague of blood. Where did it come from? Was it a natural disaster, or was it something God did magically? Meshach didn't like the word *magic*—that's what the Egyptian magicians practiced in Pharaoh's court—but there was no other explanation, so in some ways it was magic. Of course, the strange events could certainly be called supernatural.

And then there was the plague of frogs. Did they leave the river because they couldn't live in the water, or were they just part of God's magic too? And what about the next plague Aaron said was coming? What would it be?

There were so many questions waiting to be answered, but Meshach didn't have the courage to ask them. He was afraid. He was little more than a boy at thirteen, and Aaron was a grown-up. Aaron was the brother of Moses, who was now the most famous person in all the land of Egypt, besides Pharaoh.

But Meshach decided no matter how frightened he was, he had to say something. He just had to. If he let this moment pass without asking at least one question of Aaron, he knew he'd never forgive himself.

"Sir?" Meshach swallowed hard and stared at the ground. In all his born days he had never thought he would get a chance to speak with Aaron.

Aaron turned and looked at Meshach. "Yes, Son?"

"Well—I was wondering, Sir," Meshach looked at Asher and then back at Aaron, "do you know what the next plague will be?"

Aaron's face grew sad, and he got a faraway look in his eye.

Meshach almost held his breath, waiting for Aaron's answer. Would the great man share such a thing with someone like Meshach? Was it a secret? Would he tell Meshach now, or would Meshach have to wait for the public announcement after it had been proclaimed in Amenhotep's court?

"Only Jehovah knows," Aaron replied, "and His servant, Moses."

Meshach's face fell with disappointment. He would have to wait for the answer like everyone else.

But should he be surprised? The idea that he should expect Aaron to tell him such a thing was ridiculous! Such information would surely be a national secret.

Meshach could hardly sleep that night because of the excitement he felt growing in his chest. With each new plague that came, the feeling grew stronger.

The streets were fairly ringing with news from Pharaoh's palace when Meshach awoke the next morning. The sun was already up in the eastern sky.

Meshach hated it when he overslept like this, and especially when each day brought new excitement to the streets of the Goshen settlement. Meshach didn't know why he had overslept. "Maybe it was all the hard work," he muttered to himself as he stood on the rooftop looking down at the street and the messenger from the city.

"A plague of insects is on its way!" the messenger shouted as he stood at a street corner. "Moses has stretched his rod over the land of Egypt and warned that Egypt will be overrun with gnats!"

"Gnats?" someone challenged the messenger. "Why gnats?"

The messenger paused to catch his breath. "I don't write the messages," he replied. "I just bring them."

"Well, how do we know for sure that it will happen?"

"The word of Jehovah is sure!" the messenger insisted. "If need be, the very dust of the earth will turn to gnats!"

Meshach felt sorry for the messenger. The man had no doubt run all the way from the palace. Fortunately it wasn't yet the hottest part of the day. He wore nothing but a white kilt made of flat reeds that hung from his waist. As he talked, sweat dripped from his body, making pools of mud in the dust of the street.

Another messenger arrived shortly to give advice as to how they should prepare for the third plague. "The word from Moses and Aaron is that you must not wander far from your homes!" he called in a clear voice so that all could hear. "They suggest building smudge fires in the streets to keep the insects away. This plague will be severe, so prepare yourselves for the worst!"

"When will it begin?" someone shouted.

"We don't know, but soon, is all we've been told!"

The rest of the message was lost in the murmur of the crowd that went up from the narrow street below.

Meshach raced down the stairs to get something to eat. He listened to Jerusha give them instructions for the day as he and Chilion hurriedly took bites of boiled barley. "You boys had better help me get enough water in to last us for a while. We have no idea how bad things are going to get around here." Mother looked tired, and the day had hardly begun.

"Yes, Mother." Meshach felt sorry for his mother. What was it like to be a parent and worry about the safety of your children? He could only guess.

"And don't forget to bring in extra dried cow dung for the fires. And try to bring some dry reeds from the river to help us build smudge fires."

"What do we need smudge fires for?" Chilion whined. "I hate smudge fires! They stink so bad! They make my nose and throat burn, and they make my eyes sting!"

"Hush!" Meshach poked Chilion. "Mother's got enough things to worry about now without your complaining!"

Meshach's father had not come home from his work on Pharaoh's cleanup projects, so the boys worked by themselves. By late afternoon they had gathered enough fuel to burn fires for a good long while. But even as Meshach piled the reeds against the outside wall of the house, he had to stop now and then to scratch at his arms. It felt like tiny needles were pricking at his skin.

Suddenly Meshach stopped right in the middle of the street—he could see tiny insects hovering everywhere! The third plague had arrived!

"They're here!" he shouted to Jerusha as he ran indoors. "The gnats are here!"

Jerusha straightened up from the pottage she was stirring over the coals. "They're here!" she repeated in alarm. "Already?"

"Yes, and they hurt when they bite. Look at my arms." Meshach pointed to his arms, now red with scratches and welts.

Jerusha's eyes darted toward the street where she knew Chilion must be playing. "Then you'd better light those smudge fires—and bring your brother in!"

The fires were quickly lit, and before long the narrow street was filled with smoke. Meshach climbed the stairs to the roof of the house to catch a glimpse of what the rest of the neighbors were doing. Everywhere he looked people were shouting, and children were running and crying to their mothers. He could see the smoke from a thousand smudge fires throughout Goshen, and down toward the lowlands along the river he could see dark clouds of what he figured must be the tiny little insects.

"Whoa! There must be thousands and thousands of them!" Meshach muttered to himself. "Hundreds of thousands of thousands!"

But up on the rooftop the tiny little insects kept hovering around Meshach, too, and biting his neck and arms. "Keep away from me, you pesky little bugs!" Meshach shouted several times as he swatted at the almost invisible gnats. Finally he returned to the street below and the welcome relief of smoke.

Meshach's father didn't come home that night or the next. Meshach could only imagine how many dead frogs there were in the land of Egypt, and all of them would have to be gotten rid of somehow. Like his father said, if they didn't get the frogs cleaned up and burned soon, diseases would probably begin to break out all over the land of Egypt.

Eli finally did come home, but he didn't look the same. His face and neck were swollen from hundreds of little bites. Evidently his work in cleaning up the frogs had kept him out in the open where the gnats could bite him mercilessly. Meshach had never seen his father in such bad shape, and he looked so discouraged too.

By now the whole settlement was in an uproar.

"I'm going to have to go to a meeting of the elders," Eli sighed. "It's being held at Korah's home. Dathan and Abiram are calling the meeting to discuss what should be done next."

Meshach got a serious look on his face. "What do you mean, 'Discuss what should be done next'?"

Eli shook his head in frustration. "I can only imagine what the tribal elders are going to say about this plague. It's the third one, and it's obviously the worst one yet. They're angry, that's for sure! Everyone knew the plagues were going to be a curse to Pharaoh and the Egyptians—but no one thought the Hebrews were going to have to suffer so much."

"I don't like Korah," Meshach replied, ignoring what his father had said. "From what I can tell, he's up to no good."

Jerusha raised her eyebrows in surprise. She frowned and then thumped Meshach on the top of his head. "You mind your manners, Meshach! Korah is one of our respected elders from the tribe of Levi."

"But he's mean to Moses and Aaron!" Meshach ducked to avoid another thump on his head.

"That may be true, Son, but it's none of your business. And besides, he means well," she added.

Meshach sat down by the smudge fire and watched his father disappear up the street. What would happen next? Would there be an uprising at the meeting of the elders? Would they shout at Moses and Aaron again? Would everyone rebel against Jehovah? Would everyone give up on the idea of going free?

No one could fix these problems. Meshach frowned. No one except Jehovah. The question was, would He do it, and when? For the first time since the plagues had begun, Meshach allowed himself to doubt Jehovah.

And then a worse thought crept into his mind. Did Jehovah even care about the Hebrew slaves? Right now, to Meshach, it didn't look like it.

CHAPTER 17

The supply of reeds for the smudge fires had gotten low, so after dark Meshach and Chilion went to the swamps to gather more. The biting gnats were so bad during the daylight hours that most people had to stay near their smudge fires. After dark, the gnats didn't bother them as much.

"That's because they can't see us to bite us," Chilion would always joke.

The next day the gnats were just as bad. No one could get much of anything done, now, unless they did their work near the fires. Grain was pounded, bread was made, and clothes were mended all while sitting around the sooty flames.

Eli came home to rest at noon. When he was out of the house during the day, he had to wrap his face and arms in cloth to avoid getting badly bitten, but he never grumbled.

Meshach was proud of his father. It was the first time he had seen his father since the night before, and he was excited to find out what had happened at the meeting.

"The meeting didn't end up like I thought it would," Eli said between bites of bread and dates as they sat around the smudge fire. "Everyone was angry when the meeting started, and we were getting nowhere. Korah was shouting, waving his arms around angrily, and now and then getting up and pacing back and forth.

" 'The Lord's judgments are more than we can bear!' he growled impatiently. 'We don't need all this trouble! It's not worth it! I say we just submit to the will of Pharaoh and be done with it! At least we know what to expect from him!'

"Then Aaron got to his feet. 'Now just a minute!' he said. 'Are you telling me that you'd rather stay here and serve Pharaoh as slaves in the land of Egypt than go to the Promised Land?'

"Korah argued some more about all the plagues being so severe. 'We can't keep going on like this!' he shouted at Aaron. 'It's going to kill us!'

" 'Frogs and gnats are not going to kill us!' Aaron replied, rolling his eyes. 'If we're patient, in the end we'll win! Wait and see—Jehovah won't disappoint us. His promises are sure. Remember the prophecies—Father Jacob said we would eventually go back to the land of our fathers, and so did Joseph.'

" 'Well, that was then, and this is now! Who can say whether the prophecies will come to pass in our lifetimes or not? I say we settle for Egypt. Things weren't so bad when we weren't suffering from these terrible plagues!' Korah swatted angrily at a swarm of pesky gnats that buzzed around his head.

"Aaron shook his head in disbelief. 'But the Egyptians are suffering from the plagues too!' he insisted. 'We can't just give up now! We've come so far and made such progress! Pharaoh weakens more with every plague!'

" 'It doesn't look as if he's weakening, to me!' Korah wouldn't give in. 'In fact, it looks as if he's getting more stubborn with each new plague! And you know it's true, Aaron! When the gnats came, he never even admitted that Jehovah had sent them!' Korah started in again on his line about God punishing the Hebrews along with the Egyptians—how the nation of Israel would be better off being slaves in Egypt than to have to suffer through all the plagues.

"And me? I was getting angrier by the minute." Eli shook his head and rubbed the welts on his neck and face. "I mean, I'm just as bitten up and swollen as much as the next man, but the things Korah was saying were ridiculous!" Eli snorted. "The very idea of choosing to work as slaves here in Egypt instead of letting God take us to the land of Canaan—I mean, really! I'll take plagues and freedom any day! I don't care if the gnats eat my arms off, I'd still rather be a free man!"

There was fire in Eli's eyes. "Actually, it was kind of scary listening to Korah go on and on like that! I mean, he was talking blasphemy!" Eli continued. "We shouldn't be dishonoring Jehovah with that kind of talk! If Jehovah says He'll take us to Canaan, then He'll do it! He's got to— He's given us His promise—He's our only hope! Anyway, I finally figured I'd listened to enough of that, and I just couldn't keep quiet any longer!"

Meshach raised his eyebrows in surprise. "You got into a fight with Korah?"

"Well, it didn't turn out exactly like that. I didn't hit him with my fists, but I did speak my mind! I stood to my feet and said, 'If any of you elders actually think you'll be happier here in Egypt building pyramids and storehouses for Pharaoh, then go right ahead and stay!' It was strange hearing the sound of my voice like that—I couldn't believe it was actually me.

" 'If all you're going to do is complain every time things don't go the way you think they should, then you'll never make it on the road to Canaan, anyway,' I added. 'As for me and my house, we're going to serve the Lord and see this thing through!' "

Eli smiled. "And all this with my face swollen up!"

Meshach could see the light in his father's eyes again and hear the excitement in his voice. It made Meshach feel good to see his father back to his normal self, and Meshach felt proud of him. "Wow!" Meshach stared at his father. "So what happened next?"

"Well, I said that I thought we should pray that Jehovah would lift the plague—from Goshen, at least. Messengers from the palace had brought word that Pharaoh Amenhotep was no more repentant now than he had been before the plague of blood came."

"And then what happened?"

"Then I prayed. No one else offered to do it, so I did."

"You prayed?"

"I did. I was tired of everyone going back and forth, and all of us arguing like that! Prayer is the answer if we want to get things done. Jehovah is just waiting for us to call on His name."

Meshach could hardly keep still. This was more exciting than he could have imagined. His father had been right there in the middle of it all, and he had been the one to pray to Jehovah in front of all those elders. "So what happened then?" Meshach kept on.

Eli glanced around, and then silently raised his hands and face to the sky. His mouth was moving as though he were praying.

Suddenly Meshach got a strange feeling in the pit of his stomach. He glanced around too, but couldn't see any clouds of gnats hovering in the streets or sky. The gnats were gone! Meshach couldn't see even one! And then Meshach looked at his arms, and he couldn't feel any gnats biting him either!

"The gnats are gone!" Meshach stammered. "They're gone, Father!" He was so excited he jumped up and began running circles around the smudge fire. "The gnats are gone, Father! Your prayer was answered!"

And then Meshach had another thought. "Father? Are the gnats gone everywhere, or just here in Goshen?"

"We'll have to wait for word from the city, but my guess is—no." Eli's face was solemn, and yet peaceful. "Pharaoh has many more hard lessons to learn before this is all over, Son, and so do his counselors and advisors. And his priests are beside themselves with frustration. They can't lead out in their sacred temple rituals, now, because they have rashes all over their bodies from the bites of the gnats."

Meshach looked surprised. "Well, why would that keep them from going to their temples and calling on their gods?"

"Because when they get diseases or their skin begins to ooze from rashes like that, they consider themselves unclean and defiled. That's something we Hebrews understand pretty well, don't you think? I mean, when we're sick, we don't worship in public either. We don't want others to catch our sickness.

"Anyway, the priests can't worship so they can't call on all their gods to save them." Eli shook his head and sighed. "It's a shame! They actually expect their gods to deliver them from plagues like the frogs and gnats, but—"

"But they can't!" Meshach interrupted his father. "And now Pharaoh is beginning to see that his gods are too weak to do anything about the gnats, or maybe that his gods don't exist at all."

"That's right, Son, and remember, Egyptians think Pharaoh Amenhotep is a god himself."

Meshach's eyes brightened. "But Pharaoh Amenhotep doesn't have control over the gnats, and he's too stubborn to ask Jehovah to remove the plague, so the gnats just stick around."

"That's right. And the priests now feel that these plagues are the punishing hand of Jehovah upon them. They are convinced, even if Pharaoh isn't. They want Pharaoh to apologize to Moses and Jehovah. They're sure that Jehovah is offended, and that the only way to get rid of the biting gnats is to admit that Jehovah is superior to their gods."

Meshach stared at his father. "And of course they're right!" he said, getting more excited by the moment.

"Exactly. Now, Pharaoh didn't repent when the plague of blood was sent," Eli continued. "He just went into his palace chambers and shut the doors. But with the frogs, it was different."

"And Pharaoh did ask Moses to bring that plague to an end, didn't he?"

"That's right. Pharaoh begged Moses to ask Jehovah to take all the frogs away. And Jehovah did. On the very day Pharaoh chose to have them removed, they died." Eli smiled again. "Of course Pharaoh never counted on having all those frogs die and pile up around Egypt."

"What did he think would happen?" Meshach laughed out loud. "Did he think the frogs would magically disappear into thin air?"

Eli shook his head and chuckled. "Well, they could have if Jehovah had decided to end the plague that way, but I guess the Lord wanted Pharaoh to have something to remember Him by."

Meshach wrinkled up his nose and grinned. It wasn't really funny because the frogs had smelled terrible, but Meshach knew that if the whole thing could be considered a joke, the joke was on Pharaoh.

Meshach squatted down on the ground beside his father again. "So, now what's going to happen?"

"There will be more plagues to come, and they're only going to get worse."

Meshach stopped smiling. "What plague do you think will come next, Father?"

Eli sighed and laid his hand on Meshach's shoulder. "We haven't heard anything from Moses or Aaron, but my guess is that it will have something to do with the plague of frogs. I mean, with all those dead bodies lying around for so long, something has to happen. Not everyone in Egypt burned or buried the frogs in their area as quickly as we did. That's got to cause problems somewhere down the line."

Meshach's eyes grew worried. Suddenly he remembered the conversation he and his father had had when the dead frogs began to pile up all over Goshen. "Then you think a disease is going to be the next plague?"

"It could." Eli nodded. "We certainly shouldn't be surprised if it turns out that way."

"Wow! That will be hard for everyone, I guess."

"It will. There's no doubt about it. This has been a test of everyone's faith, and we're not out of Goshen, yet. We should be grateful that Jehovah answered our prayers this time, even if some did not believe. I think Jehovah knew we needed that sign from Him that He would be with us."

CHAPTER 18

By late afternoon, most of the smudge fires had burned themselves out. From all the reports coming in, it appeared that there were no more biting gnats anywhere in Goshen. And the next morning the gnats were gone from the rest of Egypt, too.

Meshach went to the royal kitchens to work with his father for the day. It felt strange working in the kitchens again after all that had happened, but it also felt good to be doing something worthwhile.

The smooth stone floor felt cool under his bare feet as he thought about the plagues that had come on Egypt. Meshach had been in this very room when the workers had learned that the Nile River had turned to blood. Even the water in the clay jars sitting around the kitchen had turned into the red sticky liquid.

And now the kitchen still smelled of frogs. Several times during the day Meshach found a dead mummified frog tucked away behind some jar of water or under a sack of grain.

He couldn't believe that there had been hundreds of thousands of them. If they hadn't been such a horrible nuisance, he might have enjoyed the whole thing a little more. He had always enjoyed chasing and catching the little green things, but of course the frogs had all died, and that had brought on the real problem—what to do with all their dead rotting bodies. Burning them had been the only thing that worked. No one had been able to dig enough holes to bury them fast enough.

But the tiny biting gnats had been the worst. Meshach would never forget the itching swollen arms and necks and faces he had seen everywhere, even in Goshen. What a nightmare! In fact, many mornings

Meshach had wakened to feel them biting him all over his body. The only way he had managed to deal with that was to sleep outside on the ground near the smudge fires, and of course there was always the problem of the fires burning low. Someone had to stay awake to keep the fires fed now and then.

And now what would come next?

Meshach pounded the grain in the stone mortar to get enough fine flour to make the batches of bread the royal tables needed. Plagues could come and go, but people still needed to eat. Meshach's father was out in the palace somewhere delivering the morning meal to the royal tables.

Suddenly Meshach heard someone shouting in the corridors leading to the kitchens! It was Saatet, supervisor of the palace servants. He burst into the room all out of breath.

"More plagues are coming!" he wheezed as he held his hand to his chest. "Will these horrible scourges never stop?"

"Another plague is coming?" someone gasped. Meshach could see fear in every eye as the kitchen workers quickly gathered around Saatet.

"Flies are coming!" Saatet groaned again. "Swarms of them! I—I heard Moses himself say it down by the river. We were at the royal family's early morning rites of worship to Osiris." Saatet was having trouble breathing now, and Meshach was afraid the man was going to faint.

Saatet looked frantically around the room, his bony body a tight bundle of nerves. "Moses raised his rod to the sky again—just like he always does before he calls a plague down from his Jehovah God!"

The man sank to the floor, his face between his knees as he rocked back and forth, hysterically. "The flies are going to cover the land of Egypt!" he shrieked. "Your homes will be full of them, and the ground will be covered with their crawling bodies! We are cursed!"

"He's right!" another voice broke in. "I was there—I heard everything!" It was Hatsuret, steward of Pharaoh's palace. "But there's more," he quickly added, as he hurried into the kitchen. "Moses said the land of Goshen wouldn't be touched by the plague of flies and that this would be a sign to let us all know the Hebrews are Jehovah's special people!"

Hatsuret looked straight at Meshach. "You're a Hebrew," he said, with a look of fear on his face. "Is this true? Have these plagues come upon us because Pharaoh has made the Hebrews his slaves?"

Meshach's eyes darted around the room. Everyone was looking at him. Saatet, Hatsuret, all the workers in the kitchen. What could he say? He knew he had to speak the truth, but did everyone really want to hear the truth?

"It's the hand of Jehovah! There is no escaping His judgments!" Seti stepped out of a storage room and into the shafts of the morning sunlight that streamed through an open doorway. He looked from one person to another in the kitchen, and then his eyes rested on Meshach.

"And He's your God!" Seti scowled. Meshach could see his fists tighten angrily. "Why must your Jehovah God torture us! We are just common people! What have we done that has displeased Him?"

No one said a word, and in the deep stillness of the moment one could have heard a pin drop to the floor.

Suddenly Meshach knew what to say. It was as if a voice was speaking inside his head, telling him what he must say. "Seti's right. This is the hand of Jehovah upon Egypt because Pharaoh will not let the Hebrew slaves go free. As long as Jehovah is ignored, worse plagues will come." Meshach looked at Seti and raised his chin bravely. "There is no God like Jehovah. He is Lord of heaven and earth, and He will have the last word. The mouth of the Lord has spoken through his servant Moses, and when Moses has spoken, it will come to pass."

Meshach took a deep breath. Where had those words come from? He had not known he even knew how to say such things.

A frown crossed Seti's face, and his jaw tightened. "Then we had better get out of here! I don't want to be here when the flies come!"

The royal kitchen emptied in a hurry as everyone scurried to get out and back to their homes. No one doubted Meshach's words. They had seen enough now to believe that if Moses said it was coming, then it would come. Moses' words were like the very words of Pharaoh himself.

And the flies did come. By late afternoon they were everywhere, and by midmorning the next day, reports from the city said that the Egyptians were in a frenzy. But in all the settlements of Goshen, not a fly could be found.

"This is wonderful!" Jerusha exclaimed. "No flies! We've never had it this good, even when there was no plague. It's as if all the flies in Goshen have left to join the swarms of flies in Tanis and the rest of Egypt!"

And then she grew quiet. "The Lord has kept His promise," she half whispered, as she lifted her eyes to heaven. "The plague has not touched us."

The next morning Meshach begged to go to the royal city of Tanis to see the sight for himself.

Jerusha shook her head with concern. "I wish you wouldn't go, Meshach. We're safe here. It's a plague and meant to be a curse to the Egyptians." She frowned, and then added, "It can't be a pretty sight."

"I know, Mother, but I want to see the effects of the plague. I want to be able to remember it for the rest of my life. I can't explain it, but I feel like I need to do this."

"That's not a good enough reason to go."

"It is for me. Maybe when I have children some day, I'll want to be able to say, 'I was there—I saw it all.'" Meshach looked at his mother expectantly. "Please, Mother?"

"Let him go, Dear," Eli said to Jerusha. "His reason is good."

She hesitated. "All right—but don't go too far into the city. And be sure and take your head covering with you. If the flies are as bad as they say, you'll need it."

And so Meshach went to the city, and he was shocked at what he saw. Never in all his life had he seen so many flies! He hadn't imagined that there were this many flies in the whole world, let alone in Egypt. They were worse than even the gnats had been! They covered everything!

Meshach held his head covering over his mouth and shielded his eyes from the thousands of flies buzzing all around him. They were in the streets, in the homes, and in the royal kitchen where he and his father worked. The kitchen was so black with them that Meshach couldn't even see the stone kneading troughs or the wooden surfaces of the tables. They were crawling on the piles of newly made bread and even in the ovens. It was terrible!

Meshach ran out the door of the kitchen and down the street, where he stumbled into the local food market—or what was left of it. Not surprisingly the marketplace was empty, but the flies had certainly made themselves at home. Piles of cucumbers and melons lay strewn about as though people had knocked them over in their haste to leave. Baskets of bread and small cakes were spilled along the hard-packed dirt street, and tens of thousand of flies were busy devouring them.

But the sight that disgusted Meshach more than anything was the meat section of the market. Sheep carcasses still hung where they had been strung up the day before. Fish and cuts of dried goat meat lay in neat stacks where they had been left, but the flies were so thick that they covered the red meat with their black bodies.

And the stench of rotting meat was terrible. Meshach felt sick to his stomach. He had never smelled anything so revolting in all his life. Even the piles of dead frogs during the second plague hadn't been as bad as this!

And then, suddenly, the flies began to land on Meshach. It was as if they had all discovered him at the same moment. They crawled into his eyes and ears and hair. They covered his arms and legs, and then they began to bite. Meshach panicked when he realized that he was their next victim!

He knew he had to get out of the city—this was more than he had bargained for! *I should have listened to Mother,* he thought as he swatted desperately at the flies swarming all around him. He raked them from his arms and legs with his fingernails, but it didn't seem to do any good. All he wanted to do now was to get back home. If he could just get to Goshen, he knew he would be safe.

CHAPTER 19

Meshach jumped out of the way as a chariot rumbled by in the narrow street. The team of sweaty black horses glistened in the sun, their nostrils flaring and manes flying. Neither the charioteer nor the important-looking official standing beside him in the chariot even noticed Meshach.

After the shock of being nearly run over had passed, Meshach suddenly decided to chase the chariot and find out where it was going. A chariot like that could be coming only from the royal city of Tanis and no doubt had something to do with a message from the palace. It had to. In fact, if Meshach guessed right, the chariot might even be on its way to the house of Aaron.

Sure enough, when Meshach caught up with the trail of dust that the chariot left behind, he found the chariot outside the front door of Aaron's home.

"The great and mighty Pharaoh orders you to seek an audience in his court immediately!" the officer commanded in a loud tone. The officer's bare back glistened with sweat, and his short linen kilt was now dusty from the wild ride in his chariot.

Aaron came to the door, and Meshach could hear the two of them having a conversation, but it was hard to tell what they were saying because Aaron spoke in low tones. After a while the officer returned to his chariot. The charioteer then spun the two horses around and raced away.

Meshach sat down in the shade and waited for some time until Aaron came out and went up the narrow dirt street. Was the plague of flies finally wearing Pharaoh down? Was he willing to talk with Moses yet, and was he finally going to let the Hebrew slaves go free? Or would worse plagues have to come first?

Meshach wished that he had the courage to ask Aaron about many things. If he had a chance to speak with him, it would be great, but Meshach didn't feel he was important enough to tag along with the famous man.

And then he remembered his conversation with Aaron just before the plague of gnats had come. It seemed like so long ago, but now the thought of it suddenly gave Meshach the courage to do what he wanted to do more than anything in the world!

In a moment he was racing up the street again, but this time he was chasing Aaron. When he caught up with the man, Meshach skidded to a stop in the narrow dirt street. "Do you need someone to run messages for you?" he asked. It all came out so suddenly that Meshach hardly had time to stop and catch his breath.

Aaron turned and pulled his head covering aside. "Well now," he asked kindly as he looked into Meshach's eyes, "what's your name?"

"I'm Meshach, son of Eli, of the house of Uzziel." Meshach's eyes brightened. "I talked to you the other day about the coming of the third plague. My family is from the tribe of Levi—just like you," he added, almost as an afterthought.

"Ah, yes, now I remember," Aaron replied. "So you want to be a messenger boy?" He stopped to study Meshach again carefully. "Being a messenger can be a good thing. We need one now and then to get messages to the tribal elders. Have you ever done this kind of thing before?"

"No Sir, but I can run fast, and I'd be willing to run with a message any time of day—if you need me to."

"Yes, well, what we're really needing now is a good scribe. One who can read and write Egyptian hieroglyphics. Oh, and Hebrew, of course."

Suddenly an idea popped into Meshach's head. "My father used to be a scribe before he started working in the royal bakery at the palace," Meshach blurted.

"Your father is both a baker and a scribe?" Aaron pulled on his long gray beard.

"Yes, Sir. Hatsuret, Pharaoh's chief steward, found out he was an excellent baker and arranged to have him start working at the royal kitchens, but he doesn't work there much anymore since the plagues have begun. He could be a scribe for you if you need him."

Meshach realized that he might get into trouble for meddling in his father's business. He hadn't even talked to his father about such a thing. What if his father didn't like the idea?

Almost in answer to Meshach's thoughts, Aaron said, "That's very kind of you, Son. Have you discussed this with your father?"

"No, but when I get home, I'll tell him that we talked." Meshach looked at his feet. He felt shy again, but he was excited at the idea of his father working for Aaron.

"And if you need me, I can write, too," Meshach added suddenly, but Aaron didn't reply. Meshach realized that he was beginning to look a bit foolish. This was ridiculous! It was certainly kind of Aaron to let him go on like this, but surely he had better things to do than to stand around and let a boy waste his time. Meshach was thirteen years old, so he was actually not considered a boy anymore in Goshen, but right now he was acting more like a boy, maybe.

But if Aaron was thinking these things, he never let on.

He smiled at Meshach. "What do you and your father use for writing materials?"

Meshach was speechless. If he thought he would be tongue-tied before he started talking to Aaron, he certainly was now! There was a long moment of silence, and then Meshach blurted out, "Oh, most of the time we use clay tablets, like when my cousin and I are practicing our writing. And I know how to make papyrus. My father taught me how to do that!"

"You know how to make papyrus?" Aaron raised his eyebrows.

"Yes, Sir. My mother and father have taught me well. My father was a scribe by trade, but like I said, he is working as a baker in the royal kitchens." Meshach stopped talking. He knew he was babbling. He bit his tongue to stop the words from pouring out of his mouth.

"Here we are," Aaron said with a smile, "at my brother's house. Rest your legs for a while. I'll be out in a bit."

Meshach squatted down on the ground in the shade. His eyes grew wide as he realized that this was Moses' house. It made his head fairly swim to think of being around people who were so important. The idea that he could be a messenger boy for such famous men was like a dream. "Why me?" Meshach wondered in silence. "How could I be so lucky!"

Suddenly Aaron was back out on the doorstep with his brother, Moses. Meshach's mouth dropped open at the sight of the Hebrew leader—he had never been so near a man of such greatness. Moses' hair was almost white—not at all like Aaron's.

Meshach wondered why his hair would be so white. The two brothers looked to be about the age of Meshach's grandfather, Uzziel, but Meshach didn't know how old that might be. He had heard that Moses was a bit younger than Aaron, but he didn't know by how much.

But it was Moses' eyes that caught Meshach's attention most. They were a light gray with hints of emerald green, and so intense when they looked at you. Meshach thought he had never seen such clear, piercing eyes.

And then Moses smiled at Meshach. It gave Meshach a strange and wonderful feeling inside. There was a quietness about this man, as if he were at peace with himself inside.

Aaron laid his hand on Meshach's shoulder and gave him a smile. "You run on home and tell your parents about your idea of being a messenger for us—and your father being a scribe."

"Yes, Sir!" Meshach was so excited that he ran all the way home without stopping. Who would have thought that either he or his father would ever get the chance to work for the two famous leaders? His father a scribe and Meshach a messenger! Meshach was afraid that any moment now he was going to wake up and find out that it was all a dream!

Meshach's mother was skeptical when she heard about the plan. What would happen to Eli's job in the royal kitchens? Would the soldiers come looking for him? Would he be punished and set to work as a stone cutter or brick maker? Or worse yet, would he be sent off to work in the copper mines of Sinai?

But Meshach's father thought it was the chance of a lifetime. "I'll do both jobs for now," he tried to assure Jerusha. "I'll show up at the kitchens as needed, and then work for Aaron and Moses in the evenings. Meshach can help at the kitchens too. He can bake bread now as well as I can.

"And besides," Eli added, "with the way things are going, no one will be checking to see where I'm working. I can't go in to the kitchens right now with the flies being everywhere, anyway. There's chaos in the city, and I have a feeling that things are going to get a lot worse before they get better."

Early the next morning Meshach was up and on his way to Aaron's house. A strong wind was blowing in from the west. Meshach squinted and pulled his head covering over his face, trying to avoid the gritty grains of sand that were being whipped up off the street. He didn't mind, though. Nothing could get him down on a morning like this. Today he would begin running messages for Aaron and Moses.

Within minutes Meshach was on Aaron's doorstep waiting to hear the latest news. He noticed that several others were there ahead of him, including Aaron's cousin, Korah.

Aaron and Moses had indeed gone to see Pharaoh, as the officer in the chariot had demanded. The flies were driving people insane! Already there had been hundreds of deaths in the city of Tanis alone, because people just couldn't stand the swarms of biting flies. Many were going crazy because the pain was unbearable. Some jumped into the Nile River to get away from the flies and then drowned. Some jumped off the roofs of buildings at work sites.

And the priests were telling Pharaoh he had to do something because the god of flies was not looking good now. How could people be expected to worship at their temples, when the god of flies couldn't even protect them from his own kind?

So Pharaoh Amenhotep was ready to talk business. If Jehovah would remove the flies, the slaves could have three days off from their work schedules. Not so they could leave Egypt, of course—Pharaoh was giving permission only to go worship Jehovah in the wilderness east of Tanis.

"It's a good start," was Korah's reaction, as he pulled on his long beard. "It's about time the old weasel let us have some time off to worship as we please!"

"Worship as we please!" Aaron replied. "While we're within the borders of Egypt!" He looked straight at Korah and shook his head. "Our worship requires sacrifices of cattle, sheep, and goats! Do you know what would happen if we were to worship as we please here in Egypt? Why, the very idea of it would cause a riot among the Egyptians like you've never seen before! They worship many of these creatures!"

"It's better than nothing," insisted Korah. "At least we'll have some days off from work and give our people a chance to rest."

"It is not better than nothing," replied Aaron, "and Moses made that very clear to Pharaoh! We'll leave the borders of Egypt so that we can worship Jehovah in peace, or we'll not leave at all!"

"You don't mean it!" Korah raised his voice in disbelief.

"I do," Aaron replied. "But it won't matter anyway, because Pharaoh Amenhotep will just change his mind again now that the flies are on their way out of Egypt."

So the flies were going to be leaving Egypt! Meshach couldn't believe his ears—this was getting interesting. He should have guessed as much with Aaron and Moses' latest visit to the royal court.

"Are you telling me that Amenhotep is still holding out?" Korah kept on.

"Moses warned us that Pharaoh would harden his heart," Aaron replied, "and now that the flies will be leaving, I think my brother will be proven right once again. Pharaoh Amenhotep always changes his mind. Why would this time be any different?"

Korah snorted in sarcasm. "Well, Aaron, I'm surprised at you, oh man of little faith!"

"And I'm surprised at you, Korah! Where is all the gloom and doom you usually want to add to every situation that has to do with my brother's leadership? Get behind us, Korah! The Lord is leading here, and it's His advice we will follow!"

Meshach wondered at Aaron's words of warning, but he wasn't surprised. And he wasn't surprised at Korah's attitude, either. He had never liked the man.

And then word did come by way of messengers from all up and down the Nile Valley that the flies had gone. A strong west wind had blown all the horrible, biting flies out into the Red Sea.

Amazing! thought Meshach. *Jehovah is in control of everything. Even the wind obeys His voice, and now the flies have to obey, too.*

CHAPTER 20

True to Moses' prediction, by evening of that very same day, word came from the palace that the plans for the Hebrew holiday were being called off. Amenhotep had changed his mind once again.

The heads of the tribes were very upset. Meshach was sent throughout Goshen to bring the tribal elders to Aaron's house so that they could have a council and make plans about what to do next.

Meshach watched the men as they all filed through the gate and into the inner courtyard. Aaron's house was larger than the one-room homes that most Hebrew families had. However, this was necessary because the tribal elders were always being called to his house for meetings. The inner courtyard wasn't large, but it was big enough for tribal councils. That was where everyone was meeting right now.

Korah was at the meeting, and so were Nathan and Abiram. Both were elders in the tribe of Reuben and close friends of Korah. Aaron was leading out in the meeting, but Moses wasn't present. Of course Meshach was not allowed into the meeting, because he was just thirteen—only tribal elders were allowed to attend such a meeting. However, from where Meshach sat outside the open gate, he could hear the elders discussing Pharaoh's latest decision.

"What does Pharaoh think he is doing?" demanded Bela, an elderly man from the tribe of Ephraim. "Didn't the flies have any effect on him?"

"Pharaoh's heart is hard because he is not open to the messages from Jehovah." Aaron's voice was calm and even. "With every passing day Pharaoh Amenhotep grows weaker—he cannot ignore the hand of God forever. Tomorrow Moses and I will visit him again and try to reason with him."

A murmur went up around the room, but Aaron spoke above it. "Hear this, you men of Israel! Stand back and see the hand of Jehovah do even more wonders in the land of Egypt! About this time tomorrow, once again you will know that the Lord is God!"

Meshach didn't hear Korah say anything in reply, but he could imagine the look on his face.

That night as Meshach lay on his reed mat under the open sky looking up at the stars, he wondered if life would ever again be normal for anyone in Egypt. He felt safe enough in Goshen, but he could only imagine what the Egyptians must be feeling. They had to be feeling pain from the plagues of gnats and flies. Many were no doubt angry at Pharaoh and his stubborn pride that was bringing tragedy after tragedy upon Egypt. And they must be living in terrible fear of what was coming next. No one knew what the next plague would be.

A Nile full of blood had been nasty, and the piles of dead frogs had been just plain disgusting! Would the next plague again be swarms of some kind of insect? Meshach tried to imagine what could be worse than swarms of bloodthirsty gnats and flies.

"Whatever comes next will probably be worse," Meshach mumbled to himself as he turned over and went to sleep.

And Meshach was right. By midmorning of the next day, messengers had arrived from the royal city with news that disease and sickness were coming. Not for the people of Egypt, but for their livestock. Cattle, sheep, oxen, and even camels and horses would not escape.

However, as in the plague of flies, once again the word from Moses was that Jehovah would not send the plague on the Hebrews in the settlements of Goshen. None of the livestock of the Hebrew tribes would suffer from the coming epidemic of disease.

When Pharaoh heard the warning from Moses, he had dismissed the words with a wave of his hand. "You're not going to get me to tremble with fear before you or your God!" he growled from where he sat on his throne in the courtroom. "I trust in Apis, the god of brute beasts! He'll protect the royal herds of livestock!"

And with that Amenhotep impatiently stood to his feet. "Leave my presence at once!" he ordered. "You have insulted the throne with such talk. The Egyptians are the favored people—not the Hebrew slaves! It was luck that there were no flies in Goshen! Your string of good luck will give out any time now!"

According to the messenger, the whole court of Pharaoh was now in an uproar. Priests, court counselors, astrologers, and even the magicians were dismayed that Pharaoh would take such a warning so lightly.

Meshach's mouth dropped open, too, and a murmur went up from the crowd of people in the street as they all listened to this latest bit of news.

"Pharaoh is going to pay for saying such a thing!" someone shouted.

"He should know better than to depend on the worship of his pagan gods!" a chorus of voices joined him.

"That's right! Jehovah will not let this pass. Pharaoh will pay."

It was good to hear the Hebrew people speaking out in favor of Jehovah, Meshach decided. Even if things weren't altogether wonderful in the land of Egypt, at least faith in Jehovah's power was growing stronger.

And then the epidemic struck just as Moses said it would. It was a deadly disease, called anthrax. It caused cattle, sheep, and goats to weaken and then finally collapse on the ground. Horses, oxen, and donkeys didn't escape either. Within three days the Nile Valley was littered with the bodies of dead and dying animals. Even the hardy camels, used for long trips across the desert, were struck with the disease. It seemed that no animal in Egypt would escape the plague.

But just as predicted, the herds of sheep, goats, and cattle in Goshen were untouched by the epidemic. They continued to graze peacefully in the grasslands of the Nile Delta as though nothing had changed in all of Egypt.

Again Pharaoh's soldiers arrived to round up Hebrew men to come and help get rid of the tens of thousands of dead animals littering the Egyptian countryside. Again Eli was called to help with the cleanup. This time it was far more difficult, though. The frogs were tiny compared to some of the large animals that had now died of anthrax.

Frogs could be moved fairly easily, but many of the dead animals in this plague were too large to be dragged very far. Cattle, horses, and camels had to be buried where they were, or at least burned.

Understandably, Egypt was running out of fuel to do the job quickly. The bodies would smolder for many days in some cases, and the Hebrew men were asked to go back again and again to try and start the fires under the charred bodies now bloating in the sun. And there was very little wood to do the job properly—the land of Egypt had few trees. In many cases reeds, and in some cases pitch, had to be gathered up and piled around the dead animals to help them burn faster.

The job was taking far longer than everyone had estimated. Meshach, along with hundreds of other young men from the settlement, was finally called to help, but there were still not enough workers to do the job quickly. Some workers were brought to Tanis, and others were sent to Pithom and Rameses, where Hebrew slaves had been working for years to build storehouses for grain and stables for Pharaoh's war horses.

When Meshach arrived at the city of Tanis, he was shocked at the sight of all the carcasses being piled up. The smell of death all around him made him feel faint. Jackals fought with one another over the dead flesh even though there was plenty to go around, and vultures sat atop the unburied carcasses now crawling with maggots.

"I wish Meshach didn't have to see such things," Jerusha had complained to Eli. "A boy his age shouldn't be called to do such a task."

Eli looked at Jerusha, his shoulders sagging with weariness. "I agree, my good wife, but what else can we do? We need manpower—these dead animals should have been taken care of days ago, but there just are not enough men to do the job."

He shook his head and sighed. "And we've got bigger troubles coming now."

"What kind of troubles?" Jerusha's eyes flashed fear.

"There's no way that this epidemic will end here, no matter what we do. The flies are beginning to increase in numbers again. It's only a matter of time before they spread disease and death to all the people of Egypt. It's inevitable."

Eli put his arm around her shoulder. "But don't worry, my dear. It's clear now that Jehovah has His protecting hand on us and our people—but I fear the worst for the Egyptians," he added.

The job of burning the dead animals or burying them took several more days. In the end, Egyptians soldiers and common Egyptian folks were working side by side with the Hebrew men and boys to finish the job.

A strange silence now filled the land. It was the silence of death. As Meshach walked the streets of Tanis, very few living creatures could be seen anywhere, except a bird now and then, or maybe a mangy dog scrounging for something to eat.

"Hasn't Amenhotep had enough?" Meshach asked his father in disbelief as they sat at home one night eating a simple meal of bread and goat cheese. "I would never have believed that all this could happen! If I were Pharaoh, I would be horrified beyond belief! If it were me, I would have let the Hebrews go just because there is nothing else I can do!"

Eli nodded his head. "I agree. There should be no doubt in Pharaoh's mind now that Jehovah is protecting us. These last two plagues have not even touched the Hebrews. We are different—we are chosen by Jehovah, and that can't look good for a superstitious man like Pharaoh."

"But he hasn't changed his mind!" Meshach exclaimed. "He hasn't repented of this madness that keeps bringing more plagues upon him and all Egypt."

"That's right." Eli closed his eyes and leaned his head against the wall of their mud-brick home.

"So what will happen now?"

"We will have to wait and see," was all Eli could say.

Wait and see. Meshach shook his head. Lately that was all anyone could do.

CHAPTER 21

Before dawn the next morning Meshach was at Aaron's doorstep. The first pink streaks of day were painting the eastern sky as Meshach pulled some bread and dates from the folds of his tunic. He had not even taken time to eat before he left the house because he was so excited. He couldn't wait another minute to find out what the day would bring.

As Meshach squatted beside the entrance to Aaron's house, he thought about everything that had happened lately. It was obvious Pharaoh Amenhotep cared little about the freedom of the Hebrew slaves, and it appeared he cared equally little for his own people. Why else would he refuse to give in to Jehovah's command to let the slaves have a few days off for worship and a celebration feast? Not letting the Hebrews go was the very thing that was bringing the plagues down on Egypt. The whole thing was getting incredibly ridiculous!

Meshach could see now that his father was right. Amenhotep was a heartless man and a cruel tyrant. Nothing was as important to him as having power over others, and he would do anything to hold on to it! He would not let the Hebrew slaves go free, and defying the Hebrew God was part of that plan. But it was becoming obvious to Meshach that by the time Pharaoh Amenhotep came to his senses, there would be nothing left of Egypt.

When Aaron came out of his house and began to walk up the street, another man was with him. The man had a short jet-black beard, and Meshach noticed that his eyes were dark as midnight, too. He was taller than Aaron, and he wore a short sword on his left hip.

Who was this stranger? Meshach had never seen him before. Compared to Aaron and Moses, he was fairly young. He seemed quiet and steady, and when he talked, his voice seemed to take charge of a conversation. He was obviously strong too. Meshach could see large muscles on his arms and chest.

Meshach hurried to keep up with the two men as they strode up the narrow street to where Moses was staying. Meshach didn't want to miss a thing. He wanted to be as near as possible to see what excitement was coming next.

The two brothers talked with the stranger for a while. When Meshach and the men walked out of Goshen toward the Nile River, Meshach guessed they were probably on their way to see Amenhotep. It was almost time for the Pharaoh's royal morning ritual at the river.

Before long the four of them stood on a small bluff overlooking the river. Meshach could see a group of courtiers and attendants at the temple—and there was Pharaoh and the queen as they prepared themselves for the service.

Meshach was wondering how close the four of them were going to get to the river temple when Moses finally spoke. Turning to the man with the jet-black beard, he asked, "Have you got the bag, Joshua?"

Without a word Joshua took a leather pouch from the folds of his tunic. Moses took the bag and reached into it, pulling out a handful of black furnace soot. Then he stretched out his hand, and as he did so, the wind caught the soot, sending it up drifting away on the morning breeze.

A handful of soot! Meshach could only wonder in amazement what surprises Moses and Aaron would come up with next.

For several minutes Moses continued to lift handfuls of the stuff into the morning air, until the group of royal worshippers at the river's edge finally noticed the four of them standing there. It was obvious they were curious as to what Moses and Aaron were doing.

Finally a messenger was sent up from the temple to speak with them. "The great Pharaoh wishes to know what you are doing," the messenger said.

Aaron turned to the messenger as Moses reached into the small leather bag and pulled out another handful of soot. "Tell Amenhotep that his heart is hard. He hasn't listened to the voice of Jehovah, and because of this, another calamity is about to fall on Egypt. The voice of Jehovah has spoken."

The messenger looked frightened. His eyes darted from Aaron to Moses and then back to Aaron again. "What calamity shall I say is coming upon Egypt next?" he asked in a voice shaking with fear.

Moses pulled one final handful of soot from the bag, tossed it into the air, and then turned to the messenger. "Tell Pharaoh that both man and beast will suffer from boils of the flesh and that cries of pain will fill the land of Egypt."

Nothing more was said. Panic filled the messenger's eyes as he turned and hurried back down to the temple.

Meshach and the three men watched as the messenger relayed their words to Pharaoh Amenhotep. *What will the Pharaoh do now?* Meshach wondered. Would he send Moses and Aaron a message that he wanted to discuss details of surrender? Would he give in and let the slaves go free?

Meshach could see Pharaoh looking in their direction. He shook his head angrily and then finally raised his hand to wave them off. It was a look of impatience he gave them, but it was also a look of arrogance.

There was nothing more to say or do—the three Hebrew men finally turned and walked away in the direction of Goshen. Again Meshach had to hurry to keep up. Again he could only wonder at the power these Hebrew men held in their hands. It was as if all Egypt lived in fear of them.

Within a matter of hours it seemed that everyone in Egypt knew about the coming plague. The Hebrews knew about it because Meshach did his part in spreading the news to the streets of Goshen. The Egyptian people knew about it because it seemed that none of them had escaped. By morning of the next day, the plague had struck.

"Come, Meshach," Eli said on the morning of the third day. "Let's go to the royal kitchens—the plague may have hit every home in Egypt, but Pharaoh and his household still need to eat." Eli laid his hand on Meshach's shoulder. "And maybe there are other things we can do to help those who are in pain."

Meshach stared at his father. He had never known anyone like his father—always so kind at heart, and always thinking of others, even if they were Egyptians.

"I don't think you should go," Jerusha announced, when she heard Eli's plan. "We don't know enough about this disease yet. If you go there, you might catch it."

"Jehovah will protect us," Eli replied. "This plague isn't about us. It's been sent to the Egyptians, and not because Jehovah doesn't want to save them. He does want to save them. He just wants them and their Pharaoh to know that He is the One True God. Right now, it seems that Pharaoh and many of his priests don't want to admit that."

"But they're pagans!" Jerusha insisted as she paused in her work of sorting lentils for the day's pottage.

"It doesn't matter," Eli insisted. "We've got to do something. I feel so sorry for the Egyptians who are suffering because of Amenhotep's pride. And who knows! If we can help them see that Jehovah is also compassionate, maybe some of them will want to worship Him."

Jerusha shook her head, not bothering to look up. "I don't think that's going to happen." Meshach could see that his mother was unconvinced. She had a determined look in her eyes. "If they had wanted to believe, they would have done it by now. They have hardened their hearts like Pharaoh! It's not up to us to save them," she added as she set a clay pot of water on the charcoal burner.

"If Jehovah wants to save them, He will, but that's not what He's done. Instead, He has sent plagues on them—five, so far, and this is the sixth!" Jerusha wouldn't give up, but she wouldn't look directly at Eli or Meshach, either.

"But it's up to us to show them a better way." Eli's eyes grew soft as he looked at his wife. "We can't just sit here and allow them to suffer and maybe even die in their sins."

CHAPTER 22

Meshach and his father went to the royal kitchens anyway. The streets were strangely silent; not a soul was out and about. When they arrived at the kitchens, no one else was there either, so the two of them worked alone all morning making bread. Later in the day they went to the marketplace to purchase some supplies for the royal bakery.

But Meshach was almost speechless at the sight that greeted them as they arrived at the marketplace. Those who had come to sell their fruits, vegetables, and meats were covered in sores, and so were the people who had come to buy from them.

Meshach didn't know what he had expected, but whatever it was, he wasn't ready for it now. "Father, this is awful!" was all he could say.

After several uncomfortable minutes, Meshach finally spoke again. "I was thinking, Father—after we've taken the supplies back to the kitchens, do you think that maybe we could go and see Seti? I haven't seen him for a long time."

"You want to see him? After how he's treated you?"

Meshach turned to his father. "Well, actually, I was wondering—do you think Seti and his mother have the disease, too?"

Eli studied his son, and then nodded. "Probably—Moses said that everyone would be affected by the plague."

Meshach swallowed hard. "Well, then, maybe we should try to do something to help them, because they live all alone. I feel so sorry for them—they don't have hope like we do. Everything's going so bad for them right now." He paused. "I heard that Seti's father died years ago in an accident at a work site. Do you know how?"

"I think he was a stone sculptor—one of the craftsmen who chisel pictures and hieroglyphics on the monuments and temples that Pharaoh builds all over Egypt." Eli paused. "They say a stone column fell on him."

"That's sad." Meshach was quiet for a few moments, and then added, "You know, Seti is always angry with me, but if we do something to help him and his mother, maybe we could make a difference in their lives."

"That's a great idea, Meshach." Eli smiled and laid his hand on Meshach's shoulder again. "Do you know where they live?"

"I think I can find it. They live not far from here."

They found the house down a back street in the poorer part of town. It was a one-room house like the one Meshach's family lived in.

When Seti came to the door, Meshach wasn't ready for the change that had come over him. He was covered with sores. Even his face and hands had red oozing boils all over them.

There was nothing Seti could do but hang his head.

Meshach was quick to try and make things more comfortable for Seti, though. "We brought you some bread and raisins from the bakery," Meshach said. "I'm sorry that you aren't feeling well. Is your mother sick, too?"

Seti just nodded his head and looked toward the mat on the floor where his mother lay.

"We'd like to help—if you don't mind, that is." Meshach's heart went out to Seti and his mother.

Seti just shrugged and turned to go back into the house.

Meshach turned to his father. "Couldn't we just wash their sores with some lye soap or something? That would help to keep the sores clean, at least."

"That would be a kind thing to do," Eli agreed.

They washed Seti's sores, and then let him do the same for his mother. By the time Meshach and his father left for home, Seti looked like he was feeling better. He walked to the door and tried to express his thanks, but no words would come out. Meshach noticed a tear on his cheek as he waved goodbye to them.

In the days that followed it became obvious that this latest plague had infected the entire land of Egypt—both people and the livestock that were left. All up and down the Nile Valley the boils brought great suffering and pain, and reports said that thousands had died. Again, not a Hebrew home in all the land of Goshen was touched by the plague.

Meshach was amazed at the change that had come over many of the Hebrews during the last several weeks. The plague of boils encouraged many Hebrews to trust Jehovah and Moses His prophet, as many were now calling him.

However, Meshach was also worried because many Hebrews were growing bold enough to taunt the Egyptians about their suffering. Meshach knew that was wrong. Several times he almost got into a fight with some of his cousins because he couldn't stand the way they laughed and made jokes about "the plague of boils that had come to punish the pagans."

And yet Pharaoh wouldn't give in. Even his priests and court officials had fled to their homes. Eli came home one evening with a report that Pharaoh Amenhotep was losing support from even his closest advisors.

"They've all left his court. It's almost as if they consider it bad luck to stay around him any longer. That's quite a switch," Eli shook his head. "Six weeks ago Pharaoh Amenhotep was a god to the Egyptians—now they don't want to be near him for fear of what's coming next."

After a hurried evening meal of pottage, Meshach stood up. "May I go up to Aaron's house and see if they need me for anything? It's been a few days since I've carried any messages for them."

Eli looked at Jerusha and then nodded his head in the direction of Aaron's house. "Go on." He smiled. "Just don't be home too late."

Aaron smiled at Meshach's eagerness when he arrived all out of breath. "Well now, Son, it's a surprise to see you out at this time of night."

"I wanted to know if there was anything you wanted me to do—are there any messages or errands for me to run?"

"Well, not just yet, but tomorrow morning I think we'll have a message for you to carry."

Meshach waited for Aaron to give him more details, but Aaron only smiled. "You'll have to wait until then to see what the message is. That's all I know. I can say this much, though—we'll be going to Pharaoh's court again with another message from Jehovah."

Aaron laid his hand on Meshach's head. Tell your father we'll be leaving before sunup. He's been very faithful in carrying out his duties. Moses and I are glad that he's been able to help us out."

Meshach smiled in the gathering darkness, and then timidly asked. "I was wondering—do you think that maybe I could go with you to the royal city? That way I could be one of the first to bring the news back here to Goshen."

"That would be fine," Aaron replied. "Just be here well before sunup."

Meshach turned and ran all the way home. He couldn't believe his good fortune—he was going to the palace with Moses and Aaron! Would the guards really let him inside? He couldn't imagine that they would. He wasn't important enough, was he? In the worst way he wanted to be there and to hear what Aaron and Moses had to say to Pharaoh. Would they announce the coming of another plague? Would Pharaoh Amenhotep finally let the Hebrew slaves go free?

But whether the guards allowed him to enter the palace or not, morning couldn't come soon enough for Meshach.

As Meshach stretched himself out on his reed mat, he suddenly had a thought. He smiled to himself as he remembered the little room with the window overlooking the courtroom in Pharaoh's palace. Maybe, just maybe, he would get to see what went on in the courtroom after all.

CHAPTER 23

The royal city appeared deserted early the next morning as Meshach and Eli walked down its streets with Aaron and Moses. There were no women hurrying along with water jars atop their heads. There were no vendors carrying their goods or produce to the markets to sell. No children played games in the streets. Meshach didn't see even one person. Were all the Egyptians still in their homes because of the plague of boils?

As they approached the gates of the royal palace, Meshach could see two guards standing duty at the main gate. They looked miserable! Meshach felt sorry for them having to stand guard when they were so sick. The open sores all over their bodies looked terrible! Their chests and faces were covered with them, and Meshach could see that if they lived, they would have horrible scars where the boils had been!

They didn't say a word as they allowed Aaron, Moses, and Eli to pass, but they put their spears across the pathway to block Meshach from following.

Meshach was a little disappointed, but he realized that he shouldn't be. After all, he hadn't really expected that they would let him enter. He was still not much more than a boy.

He shrugged his shoulders. "I'm going to the royal kitchens," he announced as he waved goodbye to the three men. "I'll see if they need any help there."

When Meshach arrived at the bakery, he quickly grabbed a tray and put two loaves of bread on it. What he was about to do was risky, but if he could pull it off, he would get a chance to see Moses and Aaron in action again. If it worked, it was worth it. If it didn't? Well, he would just have to deal with that problem when it arrived. Likely as not, the palace guards would be afraid of him, knowing he was a Hebrew boy.

No one was at the kitchens yet as Meshach quietly disappeared down the long palace corridors with the tray of bread in his hands. Now, if he could just remember how to get to the place he had been before where he had first seen Moses and Aaron, it would be worth all the trouble of trying to find it.

For several minutes, he wandered the halls looking for anything that might look familiar. Finally he caught sight of the pictures of people, animals, and chariots decorating the stone walls of the palace corridors. Meshach began to get excited. Everything was just as he remembered it from several weeks before, when he first came here by accident.

But this time it was no accident. Meshach could hear the voices again, and again he felt the hair on the back of his neck prickle as he thought about the danger of wandering so close to the palace courtroom. Meshach clutched the tray of bread more tightly in his hands. If he got into trouble, the bread would be his only good explanation as to why he was here.

And then suddenly he saw the little room. It was tucked away in a corner of the palace corridor just the way he remembered it. Meshach scampered into it and ducked out of sight so as not to be noticed by the palace guards or anyone else who might be wandering by. He breathed a sigh of relief when he remembered that likely as not, everyone was probably too sick to be worried about a Hebrew boy running around.

The voices were clear now as Meshach looked through the tiny window in the wall. Below him in the courtroom stood Moses and Aaron. Meshach hoped that he hadn't missed too much.

Pharaoh Amenhotep was on his throne as usual, but from what Meshach could tell, only one royal advisor was present, along with a few guards. And everyone had sores all over their bodies—even Amenhotep.

"What do you two troublemakers want?" he demanded as he sat there on his throne, sullen and angry.

"We have come once again to tell you the word of the Lord. Jehovah has said, 'Let My people go, that they may serve Me!' "

Pharaoh Amenhotep sat up a little straighter. "And if I don't?"

"Then Jehovah will send the full force of his plagues against you, your officials, and your people so that you may all know that there is no one like Him in all the earth." Moses stared at Pharaoh without flinching.

"The full force of His plagues!" Amenhotep sputtered. "What do you call the plagues He has already sent upon the land of Egypt! According to you, He sent the blood, the frogs, and the biting gnats, and the flies! And now He is sending these horrible diseases! Isn't this enough to show His power and might?"

"Evidently not!" Moses met Pharaoh's glare with a steady gaze. "You are a foolish man, Pharaoh Amenhotep. By now I'm sure you must realize that Jehovah could have stretched out His hand and struck you and your people with a plague that would have wiped you from the face of the earth. But He didn't—at least not yet."

Amenhotep's eyes flashed. "And why not?"

"Because Jehovah has raised you up for this very purpose. He wants everyone, both Egyptians and Hebrews, to know that Ra the sun god has no power—and neither does Osiris, god of the Nile, or Apis, god of beasts! It is senseless to worship the idols of wood and stone you have made in their honor! You know that very well, Pharaoh Amenhotep!" Moses frowned.

Meshach was surprised that Moses was doing more of the talking. Up until now, the rumors all said that Moses was too timid and shy to speak in public. Some said that he was ill at ease with the language of the Egyptians. Meshach wondered why that would be. Moses had been raised right here in the Egyptian palace.

But none of that seemed to matter, now. Meshach smiled to himself. Moses was doing the talking, and it sounded like he had fire in his veins.

"You have seen the weakness of believing in such gods," Moses continued without letting up. "And yet you have used your position of power in Egypt to take advantage of your people and their superstitious fears. Again and again you have rebelled against the Most High God of heaven and earth. You have enslaved His chosen people, and now, once again you refuse to let them go when He commands you to do so!"

Moses raised his hand and pointed a finger at Pharaoh. "Jehovah knew you would be incredibly stubborn, but that doesn't mean you are any less guilty for defying Him!"

Amenhotep snorted. "You're talking like a crazy man, Moses! Any other ruler would have done the same as I have done!"

"You're wrong!" Moses replied in trumpetlike tones. "Anyone in their right mind would have submitted to the power and might of Jehovah if they had witnessed what you have seen. And now, because you have steadfastly set yourself against the Lord—therefore—at this time tomorrow, He will send upon you a storm of hail and fire and destruction, the likes of which you have never seen in all of Egypt!"

Meshach couldn't believe his eyes or ears. A seventh plague was about to come on Egypt, and Pharaoh Amenhotep had it within his power to stop it before it came—but would he do it? Would he admit that his stubborn pride was the real reason for all of the plagues? Surely now he would give in and let the Hebrew slaves go to worship Jehovah!

"Get out!" Pharaoh roared. "I've heard all I want to hear! I can't believe I've let you stay this long!"

"All right," Moses retorted, "but if you're smart, you'll send for all your herdsmen and command that any livestock you still have be brought to a place of shelter! Otherwise the hail will fall on both man and beast, and they will die!"

Moses paused and then solemnly added, "I stand as Jehovah's witness before you. He has commanded, and it will be so!"

Moses, Aaron, and Meshach's father were leaving the courtroom now, and Pharaoh Amenhotep slumped a little lower on his throne. Once again, he had been beaten at his own game but, evidently, not yet humbled.

Meshach smiled as he watched the royal advisor hurry from the courtroom too. No doubt he was worried about any livestock he might have out in the open.

Suddenly Meshach realized that Moses, Aaron, and his father were on their way to the palace gate, and that if he didn't hurry, he wouldn't be there to greet them when they arrived. He snatched up the tray of bread and ran down the corridor toward the kitchens.

CHAPTER 24

Meshach tried to act surprised when Aaron gave him the latest message from Pharaoh, and then he ran all the way to Goshen without stopping. It was a good thing that it was still early morning, or Meshach would have fainted from the heat as he had seen some of the other messengers do.

And true to Moses' prediction, at midmorning the next day a storm hit the land of Egypt like no storm anyone had ever seen or could remember. From the roof of his home, Meshach watched the storm clouds gather on the horizon all around the land of Goshen. The sky was still blue above the Hebrew settlements in Goshen, but everywhere else the terrible storm raged in all its fury. Meshach could hear booming claps of thunder and see lightning zigzag across the heavens. In awe he watched the rain pour from the sky as if it were Noah's flood all over again.

He could hardly believe his eyes! Again it was as if a wall of protection had been drawn around the land of Goshen! It was as if Jehovah had said to the wind and rain, "This far you will come, but no farther!" As Meshach stood on the roof, wondering at the magnificent display of power in the distance, he caught sight of a chariot driving madly toward the settlements in Goshen. He watched as it careened through the streets, nearly tipping over on its side as it turned the corner on Meshach's narrow street.

Minutes later it returned down the street, this time with Moses and Aaron in it, hanging on for dear life. As they disappeared across the landscape toward the wall of wind, rain, and lightning, Meshach watched the driver give them each a metal shield to hold above their heads for protection from the falling hail.

Within the hour the storm was over. What had happened at the royal palace? Had Pharaoh finally given in? Had he asked Moses to remove the storm? Had he agreed to let the Hebrew slaves go free?

Meshach couldn't wait until messengers came from the city with the news, so he decided to run all the way there to find out for himself. He wanted to see if the damage caused by the storm was as bad as Moses had said it would be.

It was worse. Dead bodies of cattle, oxen, sheep, and goats littered the road to the city. And a few herdsmen and farmers who had not heeded Moses' warning lay along the road with them. It was dreadful to see.

And the trees and fields were damaged too. Tall palm trees were stripped of all their fronds, their large leaves shredded to bits. The fields of flax and barley were lying broken and flattened by the storm. Along the way Meshach could see that every house had some damage too, and many homes were totally destroyed, with gaping holes in their walls and roofs.

But the thing that surprised Meshach the most was the piles of icy hail that lay on the sand. The ground was almost completely white. It was a strange sight to Meshach—even stranger than the piles of dead frogs.

Meshach had never seen hail before. The stories he had heard about such storms told of hail the size of large pebbles—but now, as Meshach stood looking around him, he could see hailstones as big as leeks, and some even the size of his fist.

And hail hadn't been the only thing to cause damage. Many trees and buildings appeared to be blackened from fire! How was that possible? With rain and hail everywhere, how had fires gotten started? But as Meshach saw the stunned looks on the faces of the Egyptians and listened to their excited talk, he could tell that the fires had been caused by lightning.

Meshach felt bad for the Egyptians as he saw them bending over their loved ones who had suffered cuts and broken bones from the hail. And many were dying or already dead. A darkened sky still hung over the city as many stumbled around screaming and moaning their grief. Meshach tried to comfort some of the mourners, but he finally gave up and went on into the city.

As he did so, he met Moses and Aaron on their way out.

"There's good news and bad news," Aaron said with a smile as he patted Meshach's head.

"Are we free?" Meshach shouted. He danced along excitedly beside the men as they walked down the road to Goshen.

"The good news is Pharaoh has just confessed that he and his people have wronged us! He said he would let us go if we would only stop the thunder, lightning, and hail."

"By the looks on your faces, it doesn't look as if you believe him."

Aaron glanced at Moses and frowned. "That's the bad news. I find myself wanting to believe Pharaoh Amenhotep this time, but my brother doesn't. Moses thinks Pharaoh will change his mind as soon as he calms down. That storm gave him quite a fright. I think he thought both Jehovah and Osiris were after him that time." Aaron chuckled to himself.

Meshach shrugged his shoulders. "So let's just leave before he has a chance to change his mind, then."

"It doesn't work that way," Moses kept his eyes on the road as they walked along. "There's so much to do. Besides packing up all our things to go, we have to consecrate the Hebrew people so that they will be ready to leave Egypt. We need to be of one heart and mind as God's people. But we've been slaves for so long, I'm afraid we don't really know how to do that very well."

When they arrived back at the Hebrew settlements, Meshach was amazed at the contrast he found there. In Goshen the sun shone brightly, and children played in the streets. There were no damaged trees or fields or houses. Best of all, everybody was alive and well, going about their business as if nothing had changed in all the land of Egypt.

And in a way, it hadn't—at least for Pharaoh. Before the sun was even halfway across the western sky, messengers came to Goshen with the news that Pharaoh had changed his mind yet again.

"This is insane!" Eli protested. "Moses was right, but I don't understand! After all that has happened in Egypt, you would think that Pharaoh Amenhotep would be worn out and ready to give up! Not only has his country suffered, but he himself has been through a lot personally—especially with all the gnats, flies, and boils."

Eli shook his head sadly. "There seems to be no turning back for Amenhotep. He may think he is invincible, but the entire land will be destroyed before he wakes up from this nightmare!"

The next morning Aaron sent for Meshach and his father. Again they made the trip to see Pharaoh, and again Meshach was allowed to go along. This time they went to the Nile River, where the royal family held their rituals at sunrise.

"How long will you refuse to humble yourself before the Lord?" Moses called in trumpetlike tones from the small bluff overlooking the river's edge. Below them Meshach could see Pharaoh's worship party around the sacred temple shrine.

"My people were not meant to be slaves!" Moses continued. "If you refuse to let them go, tomorrow Jehovah will send swarms of locusts. They'll cover the face of the ground so that it cannot be seen! They'll destroy the wheat and lentils in your fields that have survived the storm, and they'll also eat any other vegetation that was left behind!"

Moses raised his rod to the sky. "They'll fill your houses and those of your officials," he continued. "This plague of locusts will be worse than anything you or your forefathers have seen since the day they settled in this land! The Lord has spoken!"

There was nothing left to say—Pharaoh wasn't going to listen, anyway. Even Meshach could see that. Moses and Aaron were simply going through the motions now, as Jehovah had asked.

The next day, Meshach went with his father to the city of Pithom to see how Eli's brother, Obed, was doing. Obed was a worker at one of Pharaoh's building sites. In spite of all the trouble the plagues had brought on the land, Obed was still not being allowed to leave the work site. The Hebrew men lived in a tent city while they were constructing storehouses for grain. Unfortunately, their families had to live back in Goshen.

Eli and Meshach ate a few bites of parched grain and cheese with Uncle Obed as they sat in the shade of his tent.

He looked old and tired as they sat eating, but Meshach thought it was discouragement more than anything else that made him look like that.

Eli laid his hand on Obed's shoulder. "Take courage, my brother. This trial is nearly over. Pharaoh is almost to the breaking point. He's still refusing to let Israel go, but another plague is coming—today. It'll be locusts this time."

"Locusts?" Obed replied. "Today? How do you know all this?"

"I've been working as a scribe for Moses and Aaron, and yesterday we were in Pharaoh's court. We heard the announcement."

"You're kidding!" Obed stared at Eli in disbelief. "You're a scribe for Moses and Aaron?"

Eli nodded his head. "Yesterday afternoon Amenhotep called Moses and Aaron to the palace to bargain with him about the grasshopper plague. He said he had changed his mind and wanted to discuss the details. He said he had decided that the Hebrew men could go to worship Jehovah— but the women and children would have to stay behind."

"And?"

"And of course Moses refused." Eli raised his eyebrows.

"So then what happened?"

Eli smiled. "As usual, Pharaoh drove us out of his courtroom."

Obed squinted at the brightness of the sun. "So the locusts will come?"

"The locusts will come."

"This is amazing!" Obed rubbed his tired eyes. "No wonder everyone throughout the entire land of Egypt is now living in fear of Moses and Aaron."

"Is it any surprise? When Moses says something will happen, it is as if Jehovah Himself has spoken." Eli bowed his head in reverence.

"So then, you think it's almost time for us to go free?"

"I do, but not quite yet. Moses is saying that only after Egypt is nearly destroyed and every family in Egypt has felt the pangs of death will Pharaoh let us go."

"Moses said this?" Obed's eyes flickered with a ray of hope.

"It is the word of the Lord."

Suddenly Meshach got a strange feeling in the pit of his stomach. He jumped up and ran outside the tent. "The sky is getting dark in the east!" he announced. "It looks like we're in for a sandstorm, Father! Maybe we'd better get under cover!"

Eli stepped outside the tent and squinted at the eastern sky for a few moments. "That's not a sandstorm," he said solemnly. "It's locusts."

CHAPTER 25

"Locusts!" Meshach looked at his father in surprise. "The plague of locusts? They're here? Now?"

"It looks like it, Son."

Meshach stared at his father. "OK—so, what do we do now?"

"Well, if Jehovah is sending the locusts, they're probably going to be pretty bad." Eli studied the eastern sky again. "They don't eat people, but just the same, you don't want to be caught out in a swarm of locusts."

A smile cracked the corners of Meshach's mouth. "They're just locusts, Father. How bad can locusts be?"

Eli raised his eyebrows. "You have no idea, Son."

He turned to his brother Obed. "We're going to have to go now, but why don't you come along with us? Things are coming apart in Egypt. After today, there's going to be nothing left around here but confusion and devastation." He nodded at Obed. "They'll never even know you're gone."

Obed looked surprised. "You really think we can pull it off?"

"I'd bet a team of oxen on it."

Meshach's father was right. Before long the sky grew dark, and an ominous whirring sound could be heard. Hundreds of thousands of locusts clicked their wings and legs together, making a hissing sound that almost roared as it drew closer. Meshach tried to shout to his father, but the noise became so deafening that it was almost impossible to hear.

When the Egyptian overseers began to run for cover, Eli and Obed darted down the road to Goshen, with Meshach following close behind.

Meshach could see the locusts landing on the countryside ahead of them. They landed on the grass, bushes, and trees along the road. They landed on the ripening fields of flax and barley that had been beaten to the ground by the hailstorm. And they landed on the green fields of wheat and lentils that were still partly standing.

It didn't seem to matter if a plant was growing or dead, green or dry—the dark-brown locusts ate everything in sight. They weighed down the grass, and even the branches of the trees hung clear to the ground.

Meshach shuddered at the sight of it all. The locust hordes looked like a big army of creeping, crawling creatures. The ground was alive with them, and he couldn't keep from stepping on them as he hurried down the road with his father and uncle. They crunched under his feet, but he tried not to think about it. Meshach was glad he wasn't a girl; a girl might have screamed.

And then the locusts began to land on him. They were trying to crawl into his clothes and his hair. They were scratching his face and ears with their prickly legs. Meshach thought he was going to go crazy.

Meshach and his father and uncle ran for a long way, but they finally had to slow down. The afternoon heat was stifling! They tried to get a drink of water from a well, but there were just too many locusts everywhere! When Meshach's father pulled the goatskin bucket up out of the well, it was filled with the insects. Meshach stared at the locusts, but he couldn't believe his eyes! The well itself was actually beginning to fill up with the squirming, crawling locusts!

How could there be so many of them? They were crawling and jumping on the ground, climbing the plants and trees, and filling the air by the hundreds of thousands as they moved from field to field! Meshach knew that for as long as he lived, he would never again see anything quite like it!

Eli finally managed to fill the leather water skin he carried over his shoulder, and then the three Hebrews set out for Goshen again.

As they neared the border of Goshen a few hours later, the locusts began to thin out, and then finally disappeared altogether. It was incredible! If Meshach hadn't seen it, he wouldn't have believed it!

When the three of them reached the settlement in Goshen, they found life there going on as though nothing had happened. It was all like a dream to Meshach. Again it was as if there was a wall somehow between the Hebrew settlements and the rest of Egypt! Goshen lay in the fertile Nile Valley and had some of the best cropland in all of Egypt, but the locusts were all strangely absent.

Meshach and his uncle lifted their faces to heaven as Eli thanked Jehovah for His protecting hand.

They ate early that evening so that everyone could go to bed. The trip all the way to Pithom and back in one day had worn everyone out. Meshach was so excited, he could hardly go to sleep at first, but being out under the stars on the rooftop helped him to relax.

He knew he needed to get some rest. With the way things were going lately, no one could be sure what the morning would bring. Would Pharaoh repent once again? If not, what tragedy would come to Egypt next? And what was it that Meshach had heard his father say to Uncle Obed? That "before the Hebrews were set free, Egypt would be nearly destroyed, and every family in Egypt would feel the pangs of death"? Well, the locusts had looked bad on the road from Pithom, but would they do as much damage throughout the rest of the Nile Valley?

Meshach finally dozed off. He would just have to wait until tomorrow for the answers to those questions.

It seemed that Meshach had barely gone to sleep when he felt a hand on his shoulder shaking him. It was his mother.

Meshach sat up quickly. The sun had already risen and was getting hot. "Why did I sleep so late?" he asked. "And where's father? Has he gone already?"

Meshach rubbed his sleepy eyes and tried to shake the cobwebs from his brain. "Is there word from the palace about the locusts yet?"

"Whoa! Whoa, now!" Jerusha laughed cheerfully. "Slow down. One question at a time. Your father asked me to let you sleep a little longer."

"I should have woken up on my own! I wanted to go with him!" Meshach protested. "Where is he now?"

"He went to help Aaron and Moses. They expect that Pharaoh will be sending for them any time now."

Meshach sprang to his feet. "I've got to go, then! They may need me to carry a message for them or something!"

"Well, come downstairs, then. I'll fix you something to eat."

"I don't have time!" Meshach insisted, as he quickly pulled on a tunic and slipped into his sandals. "They may already be gone to the palace!"

"All right, then." Jerusha sighed. "I'll get you some bread and dates, and you can take them with you."

When Meshach arrived at Aaron's house, it was already nearly mid-morning. Eli was sitting on the ground just outside the front door with sheets of papyrus laid out in front of him. He was writing messages from Aaron to each of the head tribal elders.

"Why didn't you wake me when you left?" Meshach asked his father.

"You needed the rest, Son. That trip to Pithom yesterday really wore us all out." He smiled and winked at Meshach. "Don't worry, Meshach. I know what's best for you, and I won't let you miss out on anything exciting that's going on here.

"Now, I don't know how bad the locusts are, Son, or what they're like over in the city, but I'd like you to go to the royal kitchen and see if you can be of some help there. If we come down to the city later, I'll send a messenger to the kitchen to let you know we're going in to speak with Pharaoh again."

"All right, Father." Meshach smiled sheepishly. He felt ashamed that he had doubted his father, but it was hard to be left behind when he knew something exciting was about to happen—and that was pretty much all the time now.

Meshach watched as his father continued writing messages. "Father," Meshach began as he sat down on the ground beside his father, "I've been thinking about something you said yesterday when we were at the work site in Pithom. You told Uncle Obed that real trouble was on the way and that every family in Egypt would feel the pangs of death. What did you mean by that?"

Eli put down the quill he was writing with. He looked at Meshach. "The general feeling now is that Pharaoh Amenhotep is probably not going to give in and let us go until something really terrible happens."

"Something terrible?" Meshach stammered. "Haven't enough bad things happened in Egypt, already?" Meshach shook his head angrily.

"What part of Jehovah's message doesn't Amenhotep understand? By now, anyone in his right mind should be able to see that Egypt is finished!"

"You would think so, but worse is yet to come, Meshach."

"Worse!" Meshach exclaimed. "Worse than the disease that killed all the livestock in Egypt? More terrible than the boils or the lightning and hail or the locusts?" Meshach threw up his hands. "How much worse can it all get?"

"I guess we'll have to wait and see."

Meshach looked at his father and then sighed. "I shouldn't get so upset. I guess Jehovah can take care of all this. We'll just have wait for Him to work things out."

Eli smiled and picked up his writing quill. "Those are wise words, my son. Cherish them in your heart during the next few days. You'll need them."

CHAPTER 26

Meshach went to the kitchens, but when he left the Hebrew settlement in Goshen, he had to pull his head covering over his face to keep the locusts from flying into his eyes. "This is crazy!" he mumbled in disbelief. "I can't believe Pharaoh hasn't given in yet!"

Meshach worked alone all day in the kitchens—no other workers were there. He did his best to grind grain in the stone mortar, but he kept crushing the locusts with the grinding stone. He tried to work yeast into the bread, and then bake the loaves in the ovens, but it was no use. Some of the brown crusty loaves even came out of the ovens with locusts baked right into them.

"Does it matter?" Meshach muttered to himself. "Lots of people eat locusts, so a few in the bread won't hurt any."

But Meshach could hardly concentrate. He had to keep pulling the locusts off his hair and face and out of the dough he was kneading. He finally stopped altogether and just stood in the middle of the kitchen floor with his hands on his hips. What was the point of going on? What was the point of trying to finish the baking?

There were so many locusts that they were continually hopping into the ovens, where they were burned to a crisp. And then there were hundreds more everywhere on the tables and floors just waiting to eat the bread when it came out of the ovens.

Meshach was so frustrated after baking one batch of bread that he finally decided he would just go home. Suddenly, though, he looked up to see Seti standing silently in the doorway of the kitchen.

"Hey, Seti!" was all Meshach could think of to say.

For the longest time Seti just stood there, watching Meshach work, but then he finally spoke. "I want to thank you for coming to my house and helping me and my mother when we were sick. She was so sick that I thought she might die." Seti swallowed hard. "Nobody cared. They all had their own people who were sick. Some of our neighbors who got the boils did die. One of my cousins did, too."

"I'm glad you and your mother are OK now." Meshach tried to focus on what Seti was saying and not to think about the hundreds of locusts jumping about in the kitchen.

"Yeah, me too," Seti replied. "Anyway, I've been thinking about something you said a while ago. It was the day the flies came, and we were here in the kitchen." Seti was looking at the floor now. "You said that there is no God like Jehovah. And then you said that you wished I could know Him like you do."

Seti raised his head and looked at Meshach. "So I was wondering, would your God let me worship Him too? I would do whatever you tell me I should do."

Meshach looked at Seti. Again, for a long moment he didn't know what to say. "Jehovah doesn't ask a lot," Meshach finally said. "He wants you to know that He loves you, Seti, and He wants you to live with Him someday in the afterlife. That's pretty much it. It's why we worship Him—because He is the God of the universe, and He loves us."

Meshach knew this must sound really strange to Seti. All the Egyptian gods Seti was used to worshiping cared nothing about people. People were born to serve the gods.

Seti helped Meshach finish up in the kitchen, and then Meshach walked Seti to his house before he headed home to Goshen himself. All day he had waited for word from his father about Pharaoh's court, but it never came.

The sun was going down as Meshach walked along the road toward the Hebrew settlements in Goshen. By now it appeared as though the locusts had eaten most of the vegetation. Their food supply had nearly run out, and the countryside looked like a desert, even in the rich grasslands of the Nile Delta. But the locusts were still everywhere, and to Meshach it looked as if they were just sitting around waiting for some signal to move on.

Meshach hadn't been home for long when a messenger arrived to ask him and his father to come to Aaron's house. They barely had time to sit down and eat the evening meal.

When they got to Aaron's house, they learned that Pharaoh had called for Moses. It was well after dark, but the three men headed for the palace anyway. Meshach went along with them. He carried a torch as they walked out of Goshen toward the royal city, and even in the dark he could feel the locusts crunching under his feet on the roadway.

When they arrived at the palace, Meshach waited at the gate. At this time of night it was too risky to try and sneak off to the little room overlooking the royal courtroom.

It wasn't long before the three men came back. Meshach had a lot of questions to ask, but when he heard that Pharaoh Amenhotep had begged them to pray to Jehovah so that the plague of locusts would be removed, Meshach couldn't believe his ears.

"But there's hardly anything left!" Meshach protested. "The locusts have already eaten almost everything! What's the use of getting rid of them now?"

"You've got to understand that Amenhotep is a very superstitious man," Aaron replied. "I'm sure he feels that the longer these plagues stay around, the worse each plague's curse will be."

Eli scratched his chin. "That may be true, but come to think of it, Pharaoh Amenhotep didn't mention the part about letting the Hebrew slaves go free, even if the Lord does take the locusts away."

"That's because he was just trying to buy time." Meshach could see Moses' frown even in the light of the torch. "He has no intention of letting us go. Not yet, at least."

The next morning when Meshach awoke, a strong west wind had come up. As the sun rose, the sky grew dark again, but this time Meshach could tell it wasn't a sandstorm blowing in. It was countless hordes of locusts flying over. The wind seemed to be taking them east, out into the desert. Meshach could see other families all over Goshen standing on their rooftops watching the sight too.

Meshach was so excited, he ran all the way to Aaron's house without even eating breakfast. Things were happening so fast every day now. Meshach knew no one was really surprised anymore when it was announced that a new plague was coming. Worried or frightened, maybe, but not surprised.

Egypt was slowly but surely being destroyed because of Pharaoh's stubbornness and foolish pride. Egypt's water supply was gone! The people's health was gone! Their livestock were gone! The crops were all gone! Egypt, indeed, was finished.

And yet somehow, Pharaoh just wasn't getting the message that, like it or not, Jehovah was going to win in the end. The slaves would go free!

And other plagues to come? There was no doubt in Meshach's mind now that the locusts would not be the last of the plagues. Hadn't Moses said so? The question was, What would be next? It seemed to Meshach that everything bad that could possibly happen had already happened.

Aaron was eating his morning meal when Meshach came running up the street all out of breath. The elderly man smiled at Meshach's enthusiasm when he came into the house. "Don't hold your breath, Son," he said, almost in answer to Meshach's thoughts. "We're waiting for word from Pharaoh that he's changed his mind once again."

Sure enough, about midmorning, a chariot came racing up the narrow street, stirring clouds of dust as it went. The message from Pharaoh was short and to the point. "Pharaoh decided that it's not best at this time to release the slaves from their work assignments."

And with that, the messenger wheeled in his chariot and was gone.

Meshach stared at Aaron. "What do we do now?" he asked.

Aaron sighed, and half chuckled to himself. "There's nothing to do but wait for the next plague."

"And what will that be?" Meshach held his breath.

"Darkness." Aaron handed Meshach a parchment with a message written on it. "Moses asked me to send you throughout the settlements here in Goshen with the news."

"Darkness?" Meshach felt an anxious tugging at his heart. "But darkness won't come here to Goshen, will it?" He didn't want Aaron to know that he was afraid of the dark. Darkness scared him more than anything. It scared him more than being up high off the ground, and more than fear of deep water. It scared him more even than poisonous snakes did.

Aaron winked at Meshach. "No, of course not—we'll have daylight, and then of course at night there will be darkness as usual with a moon." He smiled reassuringly. "Don't worry, Son. This message is to help strengthen everyone's faith that Jehovah is in charge. For the Egyptians, however, during the day there will be total darkness throughout the land of Egypt. At night there will be no moon or stars at all. It's just another one of Jehovah's judgments to punish Amenhotep for refusing to let us go."

Aaron finished eating his meal of barley cakes and leban and then wiped the crumbs off his lap. "You know, the Egyptians worship Ra, the sun god, so this will be especially hard for them. It's my guess that, for them, it will probably be the most frightening plague so far."

Meshach took a deep breath. He still hadn't gotten over the feeling of panic he had felt when Aaron first mentioned the darkness. "What will cause the darkness?" Meshach asked.

"We don't know yet. A sandstorm maybe. When my Grandfather Kohath was young, darkness came for several days once when a mountain of fire erupted in the great sea to the north." Aaron raised his eyebrows and shook his head. "The Lord hasn't told us how the darkness will come."

He got to his feet. "Now, let's get that message out to our people, and then come back here for any other instructions my brother may have."

"Yes, Sir!" Meshach shouted as he raced off down the street. It was great being a messenger for Aaron and Moses! He didn't especially enjoy delivering news about the coming judgments, but if the news helped give the Hebrews courage, maybe it would strengthen their faith in Jehovah.

CHAPTER 27

The heat of the noonday sun was past when Meshach began his run through Goshen to give the message that a plague of darkness was coming. In record time he returned home, surprised to find his father home so early.

"There's no use in staying on at the bakery any longer today," Eli said, as Meshach walked in the door. "No one has been eating much bread. There's still plenty of bread in the kitchen storeroom for the royal family and palace servants."

Meshach grinned. "No doubt they lost their appetite with the grasshoppers crawling everywhere on everything."

"You could be right." Eli tousled Meshach's dark hair. "That, or everyone is fasting and praying to their gods."

"I don't understand that," Meshach frowned. "How can the Egyptians keep praying to their gods? Since Jehovah has begun sending the plagues, these gods have done nothing for them. Not Apis, the god of beasts. Not even Renenutet, goddess of the harvest."

"You're right, Son." Meshach's father shook his head. "I wish these Egyptians could see the folly of worshiping gods of stone and wood. My heart goes out to them."

"Well, it's not over yet." Meshach sighed and reached for a goat skin of water hanging on a peg near the front door. "Have you heard about the plague of darkness that's coming?" He handed the water skin to his father.

"I heard the news at the kitchens just before I left."

Meshach paused. "Well—I was wondering—do you think I could go to the city and warn Seti about the coming darkness? The last time I saw him he had a lot of questions about Jehovah and our way of worship, and well—I was thinking that maybe some more talk might help him and his mother not be so afraid when the plague comes."

"That's kind of you, Meshach—I'm sure he'd be grateful. Don't be gone too long. It'll be dark before you get home, but you're a young man now. I'm not worried about you. Just remember, at the first sign of darkness—and I mean real darkness—be sure and race on home."

When Meshach arrived at Seti's house, they were just sitting down to the evening meal.

"Have a bite to eat with us," Seti's mother offered.

"Thank you," Meshach said as he took his place cross-legged on the floor around the central bowl of steaming lentils seasoned with leeks and garlic. "You're kind. I can't stay long, but I just wanted to tell you folks that a plague of darkness is coming on Egypt."

It felt strange eating a meal with a woman present. In Goshen, men and women ate separately, but with Seti being the only man in the house Meshach could see why he and his mother ate the evening meal together.

"I knew you'd probably be worried when you heard the warnings," Meshach said, "so, I came over to see if there is anything I can do for you." He looked first at Seti, and then at his mother. "We don't know how long the darkness will last," he added.

Seti's gaze dropped. "I was sure that more bad news was to come," he said, "but I was hoping it wouldn't be this soon."

"I'm sorry, but it looks like any plagues we have from now on will probably come quickly, one right after the other." Meshach dipped a piece of bread into the large bowl of pottage.

Neither Seti nor his mother said anything, but Meshach could see by the look in their eyes that they were worried already.

"Oh, and I brought you some extra bread, in case you run out." Meshach jumped up to get the bread from a sack he had left by the door. "And you will want to get a few days' supply of water in, too. My father said it will probably be difficult to find your way to the wells."

Seti sighed and then finally looked at Meshach. "Thanks for coming," he said. "You're a good friend, Meshach—more than a friend, but," and then he grew quiet again, "I was wondering, do you think that your God could accept people like us? My mother and I aren't Hebrews, but—" he looked down at the floor. "We've been doing a lot of thinking. Last night we even prayed to Jehovah—or at least we tried—to ask if we might find favor in His sight."

The Egyptian boy paused, as if wanting Meshach to say something, but Meshach only waited. As Meshach's father had often said, "It's sometimes better to let people discover truth for themselves than to tell them what they should and shouldn't believe."

Seti looked at his mother and then back at Meshach. "We—my mother and I—have decided that we want to worship Jehovah, the One True God—if He'll accept us, that is."

Meshach grinned in the gathering darkness of the small Egyptian home. "Praise Jehovah's name!" he stammered. "I can tell you, Seti, that Jehovah is glad for this day. He is not willing that anyone should perish, but that all might come to love Him and serve Him." Meshach reached over and laid a hand on Seti's shoulder. "You've made the best choice of your life, Seti. You'll not regret it."

Seti breathed a sigh of relief. "Good. Now, what shall we do?"

"Well, I guess you should just wait out the plague of darkness here in your house. Get some extra food in and plenty of water. When the darkness is past, I'll come back again, and we'll decide what to do next. And keep praying," he added as he headed out the door.

Meshach ran all the way home, and by the time he arrived, clay oil lamps had been lit everywhere. He talked for a while with his father, but then went to bed. It had been a long day.

By noon the next day the predicted darkness could be seen creeping in from the northern sky. It slowly swallowed up the surrounding horizons in every direction, but as was promised, it never came into the Hebrew settlements of Goshen.

So life went on as usual for the Hebrews. People still went about their daily chores as though nothing was happening just a short distance away in the Egyptian cities and countryside of the Nile Delta. Chilion and the other Hebrew herd boys ran with the goats, Meshach's mother set a new batch of bread out to rise, and Kezia was now working on a new garment for her likely betrothal.

Although Meshach's family had been planning Kezia's betrothal, no one knew when it might take place. Everything, it seemed, had been put on hold because of the plagues. However, the message had gone out from Moses and Aaron that, as much as possible, life was to go on as usual.

Messages came from the city that the darkness was so deep it was like a blanket. No one could move about for fear of getting lost in the darkness. Even at high noon, the sky was black as midnight with no moon or stars to be seen.

On the third day, Meshach went to Aaron's house to see if there were any messages for him to carry. Meshach's father was there writing down the details of all that had been happening in the capital city and in the settlements of Goshen.

At Aaron's direction he had written about the morning the Nile had turned to blood. He had told about the hundreds of thousands of croaking frogs that had invaded the land and gotten into everything. He had described how miserable everyone was when the biting gnats and swarming flies came. And then there was the anthrax disease that had killed most of the livestock in Egypt—he told about that too, and the boils that made every man, woman, and child in Egypt sick.

But Meshach's father also recorded the fact that only the first three plagues had come upon both the Egyptians and Hebrews. After that, the land of Goshen had not been touched by the rest of the plagues. Not the flies, not the anthrax, not the boils or hail storm or locusts. And now, not the darkness. The story was shaping up, and Meshach's father was copying it all down on sheets of papyrus so that no one would forget.

There were stacks and stacks of the papyrus sheets. To make papyrus paper, reeds had to be gathered, cut into flat strips of equal length, and woven together in a mat. Then these square mats were soaked in water and pressed together between two boards. If it hadn't been for Meshach's help in making the paper, there would never have been enough of the sheets to record all that Eli needed to write down.

Meshach knew this was important. Moses and Aaron wanted children and grandchildren to hear about it for generations to come. They wanted everyone to know the events of Israel's last days in Egypt and the plagues that had brought deliverance for a nation in slavery.

"And that day will come," Eli said, as Meshach sat down on the ground beside him, watching his father write the Hebrew words to the stories. "Our deliverance is at hand, Son—even at the door!" Eli raised his eyes to heaven. "Praise be to Jehovah who gives life and help to those who ask for it in their time of need."

Eli reached for another sheet of papyrus. "And now, Meshach, you'd better check with Aaron because I think he has some messages for you to deliver."

Meshach jumped to his feet and hurried into the inner courtyard, where he found Aaron sitting with several tribal leaders discussing the plague of darkness.

"It's not a sandstorm, is it?" Sithri asked. Sithri was a cousin of Aaron and Moses.

"It doesn't look like it." Aaron glanced around the group. "If it were, I'm sure my brother would have called it that. Up to now all the other plagues seemed to have explanations, except the plague of blood, of course."

"Well, if it's not a sandstorm, what else can it be?" asked Shimei, another Levite elder sitting in the circle.

"Good question, and I've been giving it a lot of thought." Aaron stroked his beard. "Now, if you'll remember, the clouds of darkness gathered on the horizon to the north first."

"That's right!" Shimei quickly agreed as he sat up a little straighter. "The darkness did come from the north."

"My father has an idea that it isn't anything like a sandstorm at all," Aaron continued. "He said that long ago, when he was just a little boy, a mountain out in the Great Sea erupted. According to all the stories that came from the sailors in the seaports, the mountain blew smoke and fire into the sky for days. And the sky grew dark—it got dark just like the messengers say it is now all over the land of Egypt."

Meshach was so fascinated by the conversation that he forgot to let Aaron know he was standing there, waiting to carry messages for him.

"Meshach!" Aaron turned and finally noticed Meshach. "I didn't see you standing there, but I'm glad you've come. I have a message for you to deliver to the Hebrew settlements throughout Goshen. It's nothing serious—just a message of encouragement to the people." He handed Meshach a sheet of papyrus with Eli's writing on it.

"Yes, Sir!" Meshach jumped up and trotted off down the street without another word.

When he returned several hours later, it was nearly sunset, and his father was putting away his writing materials. He handed Meshach a piece of bread and a slice of melon. "Why don't you sit down and have a bite to eat? You've walked a long distance today." He patted the ground beside him and smiled. "Of course I know walking all that way isn't hard for a healthy young man like you."

"Why don't we just go home and eat?" Meshach looked at his father expectantly.

"I can't. I've got to go to Pharaoh's court in the next few minutes with Aaron and Moses. A messenger from the court arrived not long ago and told us Pharaoh Amenhotep wants to see us immediately." Eli looked at his son. "And—well—I was sure you would want to go along."

Meshach looked at his father, excitement in his eyes.

"Of course, if you're tired, you could just wait here and—" Eli paused and smiled as he reached for a piece of melon.

"No, that's OK!" Meshach began to quickly eat his own melon. "I want to come with you!"

Eli smiled again. "I thought you might."

CHAPTER 28

Meshach knew it was still daylight when he and his father left Goshen with Moses and Aaron. But as they walked toward the royal city of Tanis, the sky began to get darker. Where the darkness began, it was hard to say. It just gradually grew darker until it was so dark that even the torch Meshach held high over his head barely lit the road in front of them. The air felt heavy, and it was hard to breathe. Finally the men took off their head coverings and dipped them in water from their water skins. Wrapping the wet cloths across their mouths made it a little easier to breathe.

It was spooky for Meshach to wait at the palace gates by himself. He didn't have the courage to sneak off and watch the meeting with Pharaoh from the small room overlooking the royal courtroom. Who knew what strange and shadowy dangers were watching him out there! Meshach shuddered! It was better to be safe and stay where the three men had left him.

When the three men finally returned from their visit in the palace courtroom, they all looked serious. "Well, I guess that's that!" Aaron chuckled.

"Is he going to let us go?" Meshach looked at the men excitedly.

Aaron shrugged. "The answer is Yes and No." He shook his head. "This time Pharaoh Amenhotep said we could take our families with us, but that we have to leave our livestock behind. He says that if we take all our cattle, sheep, and goats, they'll have no livestock left at all in Egypt!"

Aaron chuckled again. "I can see his point. Tens of thousands of animals died in the plague of anthrax, and then many more died from the plague of boils! And now, what few animals they had left after all the disease have probably been nearly wiped out by the hail!"

"But—but, that's ridiculous!" Meshach sputtered as he held the torch high over his head and looked at Aaron's face. "Do you mean to tell me that Amenhotep is still trying to run the show after all Egypt's been through?" Meshach couldn't believe his ears. "Doesn't he know that Jehovah is in charge?"

"Evidently not." Aaron smiled. "Anyway, he said that we're not to come back to the court again—if we value our heads, that is."

"You mean he's going to have you all executed?" Meshach's eyes grew wide with fear.

"No, he's not going to execute us." Moses gave Meshach a tired smile and placed a hand on his shoulder. "That's just his way of talking big so he won't look weak."

Moses chuckled to himself. "If he calls me again, I'll go, but I'm certainly not going to go uninvited." He shook his head, and then added. "It doesn't really matter much—I've only got one more message for him anyway."

"Well, how will you get the message to Pharaoh if you don't deliver it in person?"

"Oh, I'm not worried about that," Moses winked at Meshach in the light of the flickering torch. "God will provide a way."

Meshach felt somewhat reassured by Moses' words, but he was still angry. It was hard for him to calm himself down as they began the long walk home. What was wrong with Pharaoh? Was he insane? He had to be, at least a little bit, anyway! What other explanation was there for his stubbornness in refusing to let the slaves go free? Egypt was in shambles, and still Amenhotep clung to the idea that he could stand up against Jehovah, the God of all nature, whom he claimed he didn't know!

On the other hand, Moses had said there was only one more message for Pharaoh. What did that mean? Was the long wait almost over? Meshach's heart beat faster at the thought of the exciting days that lay ahead.

The next day dawned bright and clear. Even the horizons in every direction were blue. Meshach slept late again, but when he awoke, his chest hurt. Evidently whatever he had breathed the night before was still inside his lungs.

When Meshach went to Aaron's house later that morning, Aaron was waiting for him.

"I have a message for you to deliver to the head elders of the tribes. Please read it in the presence of each of them." Aaron handed Meshach the sheet of papyrus. "Can you give that message to all the settlements here in Goshen before dark?" Aaron smiled at Meshach's excited face.

"I think so." Meshach thought for a moment. "There are twelve tribes, but actually thirteen, because Ephraim and Manasseh are considered half tribes. I've got to deliver your message to the heads of all those tribes, and—then probably to several elders that are tribal chiefs second in command to the heads. Is that right?"

Meshach waited expectantly. More than anything he wanted to please Aaron. Meshach knew that as long as he lived, he would be grateful for the chance he had been given to work with Aaron and his brother Moses, now the most famous man in all of Egypt.

"You're exactly right," Aaron gave Meshach a broad grin. "I couldn't have said it better myself. Now hurry along. We've got lots to do before tomorrow."

"What happens tomorrow?" Meshach stopped long enough to ask yet another question.

"Hurry along!" Aaron repeated. "We don't have time for more talk right now."

By nightfall, all the chief elders of the twelve tribes began to arrive at Aaron's house. Korah had come, and so had Dathan and Abiram. Meshach looked for Joshua in the crowd and finally spotted the dark-bearded man. He certainly looked like a leader in his dark blue tunic with a wide leather belt around his waist. A sharp saber was tucked into his belt, and he walked as if he were a military general.

The men arrived in bunches of two and three, talking among themselves quietly as though something big were about to happen. There was an excitement in the air that made the back of Meshach's neck tingle. He was not allowed to enter the courtyard where the meeting was being held, though he had been in the courtyard many times. Meshach guessed that about fifty or sixty men had come for the meeting. For all of them to sit in the courtyard, they would have to sit cross-legged close together on the ground.

Meshach strained his ears and managed to catch snatches of what the voices were saying as the sounds drifted down the passageway to the front gate.

"The day of salvation is at hand, my brothers," Moses began. "The Hebrew tribes are on the verge of a great exodus from Egypt, but not before one final plague must come."

Not a sound could be heard in the courtyard as the tribal leaders sat listening to Moses' latest announcement. Gone were the voices that had doubted Moses' predictions about the freedom promised to the Hebrew people. Gone were the complaints of having to endure a few plagues that had tested their faith and confidence in Jehovah.

"Pharaoh Amenhotep is now past the point of no return," Moses continued. "I don't believe he can see his way clearly in any decision he must make for his people—it is obvious that he thinks only of his own reputation and what he will lose if he lets his Hebrew slave labor go."

Moses sighed as though he were both tired and sad. "Pharaoh's stubborn pride is going to be his final downfall, and, in the end, I believe he will give Jehovah no choice but to go through with this final plague."

"And what will this final plague be?" Meshach heard a voice say. It sounded like Korah, Moses' cousin.

"It will be a plague of death that can be compared to nothing like it before. All the firstborn in Egypt will die, from the firstborn of Pharaoh who sits on the throne, to the firstborn of the maidservant who sits grinding grain. And then Pharaoh will let us go—in fact, he'll fairly drive us out of the land."

There was a long moment of silence, and then a distinct voice spoke again. "This is good! I'm glad to see Pharaoh and his people suffer! After all these years of slaving away in his copper mines and building his great temples and cities, we will be free! Now Pharaoh will finally get what he deserves! Real pain!" The voice was harsh, the words bitter and filled with hate.

"This is no time for anger and revenge," Meshach heard Moses say. "The Lord is good, and for those who serve Him, He works things out for the best. If all the firstborn in Egypt must die as part of Jehovah's judgments, so let it be, but let's not be glad for it."

CHAPTER 29

Meshach could hardly contain his excitement as he sat listening to the conversation that came down the short passageway from the inner courtyard.

"When will all this take place," a strong voice said, "and what will be the sign that we will be safe from this plague of death?" Meshach couldn't tell who had spoken. The voice spoke with authority as though he were already a leader among the tribes of Israel—but Meshach couldn't remember who he was by the sound of his voice, and he didn't think he had ever met the man. He knew it wasn't Joshua.

Meshach smiled to himself. He was getting good at this guessing game. Often he listened to conversations inside the courtyard. It gave him valuable information about all the latest news in the settlements and in the streets of the capital city of Tanis. Meshach knew it was wrong to eavesdrop, but every time he told himself he shouldn't be doing it, he always decided that it wasn't hurting anyone.

"Those instructions will be given to everyone shortly," Moses replied, "but in the meantime, the Lord is asking that we do something I know many have wanted to do for a very long time." There was a long pause before Moses added, "Everyone is to go to his neighbor and ask for payment for all our years of slavery."

A rumble of excited voices went up from the group of men gathered in the courtyard. "Payment?" Korah exclaimed. "What kind of payment? And how much?"

"Whatever they will give you. Pieces of jewelry would be a start. Silver, gold, precious stones like rubies and emeralds. Have the people ask the

Egyptians for bracelets and rings and necklaces. Ornaments of any kind—it doesn't matter. You can even ask for dishes or cups or mirrors that are made of brass. The Egyptians are not going to refuse anyone what they ask. Have the men as well as the women go door to door asking the Egyptians for these things."

As Meshach listened from the shadows outside the wall, he could almost see the smile on Moses' face. "Hey! This isn't my idea," he heard Moses chuckle. "The Lord has given us instructions to do this!"

The eager voices rose again on the evening air. To Meshach, this was as exciting as anything that had happened in Goshen yet.

The next morning when Meshach showed up at Aaron's door, Joshua was also there waiting, and another man was with him. When the men talked with Joshua, Meshach remembered his voice. He was one of the men that had spoken at the meeting the night before. His name was Caleb, from the tribe of Judah, and he looked to be about the same age as Meshach's father.

That morning Aaron sent Joshua and Caleb out to begin organizing the Hebrew tribes for the trip out of Egypt. They were to instruct the people as to what they should take with them and what they should leave behind. Sacks of grain and baskets of food would be easy to carry on the backs of donkeys, or in a two-wheeled cart, if a family had one. They would also need to take useful things like wooden kneading troughs. That way they could keep making bread while they were on the road to the Promised Land. And, of course, they would be taking their flocks of sheep and goats, and their herds of cattle. Though the plagues had destroyed almost all the livestock of Egypt, the Hebrew animals had escaped sickness and death.

It was also Caleb and Joshua's job to help the tribal elders choose leaders of thousands and hundreds. For two days Meshach went along to run errands for them and to carry messages when and where they were needed.

It wasn't long before Pharaoh and all Egypt had heard the rumors of the final plague. Moses and Aaron were once again called to Pharaoh's court to answer his questions. Meshach was too busy to go along, but he could imagine what Amenhotep would look like on his throne and what he might say. That was the advantage Meshach had now, ever since that first afternoon when he had witnessed the meeting between Moses and Aaron as they asked Pharaoh to let the slaves go free.

And now, of course, the story was that Pharaoh Amenhotep was furious about the news of a tenth and final plague—furious and out of control. But Moses was beginning to lose his patience with Pharaoh, too. For weeks Moses had been patiently working to get the slaves freed, but nothing had seemed to work. Meshach wondered when Pharaoh would wake up and see how ridiculous this whole charade had become!

A pattern had developed in the court of Pharaoh, and everyone could see it as plain as the hooked nose on Amenhotep's face. Moses would demand the release of the Hebrew slaves—and Amenhotep would always deny the request. Moses would warn Amenhotep that another plague was about to hit Egypt—and Amenhotep would send Moses and Aaron away. The plague would then come with all its force—and Amenhotep would either ignore it or finally repent and call Moses to ask God to remove the plague. God would remove the plague according to Amenhotep's request—but then Amenhotep would harden his heart yet again and refuse to free the slaves.

At first Meshach had been discouraged by this circle. It had seemed that things would never change—the Hebrew slaves would never be set free. But as time went by, Meshach got used to Pharaoh Amenhotep's nonsense, as his father called it. He could see that Pharaoh could not go on forever like this. He was stalling for time. Eventually he was going to weaken. He had to. Sooner or later the plagues would get so bad, he'd have to give in—that, or else his whole world would come crashing down.

But it didn't really matter what Meshach thought about Pharaoh's stubbornness. All he could do was watch and pray and continue to run messages whenever and wherever he was needed.

And things had changed some—now Moses was speaking out more against the Pharaoh. It was wonderful to see Moses in charge. When he had first come to Egypt to demand the release of the Hebrew slaves, Moses came humbly, asking that they be allowed to go free. He had been timid and almost afraid to speak to Pharaoh in public. Back then Aaron had done most of the talking.

But things were different now. Now Moses did most of the talking, and everyone in Egypt feared him and respected him. Since everything he said always came true, both Egyptians and Hebrews had come to consider his words as the very voice of God.

And that was why no one was afraid to go to the Egyptians and ask for jewelry and other valuable things as payment for all their hard years of work. Meshach's mother and sister went door to door, and Chilion even went along to carry the basket to hold all the things they would be taking home.

Preparations for the final plague were now shaping up. The plague would come on their final night in Egypt, but how exactly it would come was the big question on everybody's mind. And how were the Hebrews to escape death?

Meshach worried about that. Kezia was the oldest child in Meshach's family, and Meshach's father, Eli, was the oldest child of his family. Every time Meshach thought about it, his heart would start to beat faster, and he would begin to sweat. What would happen to Kezia and Father on the night of the terrible plague to come? Moses had promised that Jehovah would make a way of escape for every Hebrew who trusted in Him.

And that was another question Meshach had. Did being a Hebrew mean something here, or was it faith in Jehovah's power that would save them? It scared Meshach a lot when he thought about it that way, because what if their faith wasn't strong enough?

Meshach's faith began to waver as he thought about the plague of death to come. How could faith be enough to save them? It seemed that there must be something they must do to show Jehovah that they trusted Him, but what it was Meshach didn't know.

CHAPTER 30

Meshach got his answers on the second night after the announcement about the plague of death. This time even more elders showed up at Aaron's house for final instructions. Meshach's father was at the meeting as usual to record anything important that might be said in the tribal council. Meshach wished with all his heart that he could be inside the courtyard, but he knew he had to wait outside as he had done before. Only the chief elders of the tribes could be in there.

Meshach listened with his sharp ears. The things he heard made him tingle with excitement and yet tremble with dread. He was excited that his people were about to be set free, but he also felt afraid that so many people were going to die.

"Jehovah is about to do a very strange thing," Moses said as the meeting began. Not a voice or even a whisper could be heard as everyone listened to Moses' solemn words. "It is not like Jehovah to bring death in this way, but the wages of sin is death. Mercy is about to run out for Pharaoh Amenhotep and his people. They have enslaved Jehovah's people for generations, and now even with this terrible plague coming as their punishment, Amenhotep refuses to repent of his evil ways.

"But God will protect His people," Moses continued. "As surely as He has brought judgment on Egypt, He will also provide a way of escape for us, His people." Moses' voice grew stronger.

"Hear this, you men of Israel! As leaders of your people, you are to instruct every family to choose a lamb that is perfect and without blemish. The head of each household is to kill the lamb and catch some of its blood in a bowl. Then he is to take a branch of hyssop, dip it in the blood, and sprinkle the blood on the two doorposts of his home and on the beam above the doorway.

"Do this in the late afternoon before the sun sets, and then roast the lamb over an open fire. Serve the lamb with bitter herbs and unleavened bread. Eat the meal while standing. Afterward, don't undress for bed, and stay in your houses until the night is past." Moses' voice rang out confidently. "At dawn we will be leaving Egypt for the Promised Land."

"Can a goat be used instead of a lamb?" someone asked.

"Yes, the Lord will accept that."

"And what if a family is too poor to own a lamb? What should be done for them?"

"That's a good question," Moses replied. "If a family is poor and cannot afford a lamb, two families can get together and share a lamb. The Lord doesn't want to make this difficult or impossible for anyone. Just make sure there is enough for everyone to eat."

A ripple of excited voices rose on the evening air, and Meshach thought the tribal council was over, until he heard Moses speak again. "My brothers, from this day forward, for generations to come, you are to tell your children of this great night of deliverance. The memory of this day will forever be celebrated as the Passover Feast. We will always do it on the fourteenth day of the month of Abib. The lamb we kill will be called the Passover lamb, for when the Lord sees that you have put the blood on the doorpost of your home, death will pass over you."

A solemn hush again filled the air as Moses added, "And remember, the firstborn are not to leave their homes until the plague has passed. Jehovah is not willing that any should perish, but if a firstborn should leave the security of his home before the Lord has given us the signal, the blood on the doorpost cannot protect him! Salvation is possible for all, but only if we obey."

Suddenly Meshach's heart almost leaped out of his chest as a terrible thought popped into his head! What about Seti and his mother? What would happen to them on the night of the tenth plague? Would they die? Seti was a firstborn child—and Meshach didn't know whether Seti's mother was a firstborn or not.

But even more important, was it possible for an Egyptian family to escape the tenth plague of death? They were not Hebrew—did that make a difference?

Meshach jumped to his feet and began to pace back and forth. His young mind began to race as he thought about Seti. There had to be a way of escape for him and his mother! There just had to be!

And then Meshach stopped his pacing, and he stood there in the street thinking. Was it possible for an Egyptian to stay in a Hebrew home for safety? He hadn't heard anyone ask that question inside the inner courtyard.

Suddenly Meshach wanted to run through the front gate and down the passageway to the inner court. He wanted to ask the group of tribal elders that very question, but he knew he didn't dare. A young man his age was not allowed inside such meetings.

Meshach noticed Joshua standing in the passageway to the inner courtyard, and that gave him an idea. He knew he couldn't go into the meeting, but if he could get Joshua's attention, maybe Joshua could ask Moses the question for him. Meshach gave a soft high-pitched whistle, and when Joshua turned his head, Meshach motioned for him to come out to the front gate.

"Did Moses say what is going to happen to those Egyptians who have decided to follow the One True God?" Meshach began, as Joshua came out into the street. "If they believe in Jehovah's power, can they be saved too?"

Joshua nodded his head thoughtfully. "That's a good question, Meshach. I guess I don't know the answer."

"Could you go into the meeting and ask for me? It's really important. You see, I have a friend that I used to work with in the royal bakery."

Meshach paused. Would Joshua care about one Egyptian boy and his mother? The Egyptians were enemies of the Hebrews. They had enslaved the Hebrews for decades.

But it was only a fleeting thought. Meshach knew he had to give it a try—he just had to. He didn't see any other way to save Seti from certain death in the final plague.

"He's an Egyptian!" Meshach raced on. "Anyway, he and his mother told me that they now believe Jehovah is the Creator of all heaven and earth. So I was wondering, what's going to happen to them?" Meshach knew he was rattling on and on and sounded like a child.

"I'll see what I can find out," Joshua nodded before turning to go back inside.

Meshach listened for some time before he heard Joshua ask the question, and when he did, a murmur went up from the group of men sitting inside the courtyard.

"The Egyptians have no part in this!" shouted a voice. "They are pagans and deserve only punishment from Jehovah! They should not be given any mercy!" Meshach could tell it was Korah talking. Again he was angry—whenever Korah spoke, it always seemed he was angry.

A score of voices joined with Korah in protest, until Moses' voice could be heard above the rest. "Brothers! Please! Listen to me! We are being freed from lives of slavery. The Lord has taken pity on us and has showed us His mercy. Shouldn't we also be showing mercy to those who would choose to follow Jehovah?"

A silence filled the open courtyard, and then Moses' voice rang out loud and clear. "I think we know our duty! If a stranger comes to seek shelter in our homes, whether it is one of our own people, or an Egyptian who has chosen to follow the One True God, we should show him hospitality and accept him! We have no other choice!"

Meshach was so excited he could hardly wait for his father to come out of the meeting. A new idea was racing through his mind.

"Father," Meshach began, as the two of them walked home together after the tribal council, "do you think that Seti and his mother could come stay with us? They want to worship Jehovah as the One True God. They want to be a part of God's chosen people." Meshach grew more excited. "If they stay with us, they would be safe because of the blood we are going to put on the doorpost!"

Eli looked at his son. "Then you heard what Moses told the elders tonight at the meeting?"

"I did—I'm sorry Father, for listening." Meshach hung his head, and then added, "But, Father, even before the meeting I was wondering whether it was possible. Isn't that what we are supposed to do?" His eyes grew bright. "Aren't we supposed to invite people to worship the One True God?"

"Absolutely, Son—and yes, I think that would be a good idea. Let's go tomorrow and ask them to come and stay with us." Eli smiled at his son in the darkness.

"On that day in the royal kitchen several weeks ago, when you told Seti about Jehovah, I was proud of you. And I was wondering if, in the end, you might have a part in bringing Seti to the One True God."

When Meshach and his father showed up on Seti's doorstep the next morning, Seti's mother was so happy to see them that she burst into tears. In humble gratitude, she quickly knelt down in the doorway of her home. She put her forehead on the ground in front of Eli and took his feet in her hands. "My name is Amena," she said between sobs. "Let me humbly offer myself as your handmaid."

Meshach thought that was a strange thing for an Egyptian to say to a Hebrew slave.

Eli took her by the hand and raised her to her feet. "That's not necessary," he assured her. "We come to you in the name of Jehovah and from the goodness of our hearts."

Amena began to calm down. "You don't know how relieved we are to see you!" she said as she stood with her head bowed. "We have been praying to Jehovah the best we know how, but I was afraid He wouldn't hear us." Her voice faltered, as she gulped back the tears before adding, "And why should He? We know nothing of Jehovah, and Pharaoh has enslaved your people for generations!"

A faint smile of hope flitted across Seti's face, and then he quickly added, "We thought about how you came to help us when we had the boils. We're your enemies, Meshach, and yet you still came and helped us. We couldn't believe Hebrews would do that for Egyptians! Not after the way our people have treated your people!"

Meshach thought he saw tears in Seti's eyes, too, but he wasn't quite sure.

"Anyway, I kept telling Mother, 'Meshach won't forget about us. He'll come back and help us. He won't leave us here to die!'"

"And we won't." Eli swallowed hard to keep back his own tears. "You can come stay with us. The final plague will come in a few days, but you'll be safe because of the blood we are going to put on our doorpost."

Seti and his mother looked confused. They glanced at each other and then at Meshach and Eli.

"Go ahead and get your things together," Eli urged them. "We'll explain it all on the way to Goshen."

CHAPTER 31

For three days Meshach and his family prepared for what Moses promised would be their last night in Egypt. They packed everything they would need for the journey out of Egypt. There wasn't much to take with them, but there wasn't much to leave behind, either.

The basic Hebrew home had little in it. There were the baskets of food and the few cooking utensils women used every day—things such as clay pots and bowls and kneading troughs for bread. And there were the few tools men used to tend their crops—such as hoes and winnowing forks for the harvest. But other than the one or two sets of clothing a slave might own, there was little else.

And before the Hebrews left Egypt, they needed to prepare for what Moses and Aaron were calling the Passover Feast. It would be eaten on the last night before they left Egypt.

Seti's mother, Amena, helped Jerusha and Kezia make the unleavened bread from flour and olive oil. The women also gathered bitter herbs from their small gardens, as Moses had instructed the families to do.

During the late afternoon of the third day, Meshach and Seti helped Eli catch one of the lambs from their small flock of sheep. A lump came up in Meshach's throat as he and Seti brought it to the family doorstep. Meshach hated to see the lamb die, but he knew it was necessary. He had seen lambs die before in the family ceremony. He knew the ceremony represented the death of the Savior who would one day come and pay for the sins of all those who believed in Him. But this time it somehow felt different.

This time it meant that the lamb was dying to save the lives of family members right now, in a very real way—not just sometime in the future.

The lamb's blood on the doorpost would keep the plague of death from entering their home. If it weren't for this lamb's blood, Kezia and Meshach's father would die—they were firstborns in their families. There was no doubt in Meshach's mind that such a thing could happen.

So now the lamb must die. There was no other way. It made Meshach shiver as he held the wooly creature tight in his arms and watched his father pull the knife across the little lamb's throat. Meshach's arms trembled as the life flowed out of its little body. He felt numb as he saw his father catch some of the blood in a clay bowl.

Meshach knew he was not a boy anymore at thirteen. He was considered a man, but the ceremony wasn't getting any easier every time it happened. It was getting harder.

A tear trickled down Meshach's face. Maybe it was because he knew what the sacrifice meant. Maybe it was because he more fully understood that this lamb represented the price Jehovah would have to pay for Adam's sin and the sins of all those who had come after him. Meshach knew that the promise had been given since the creation of the world that Jehovah Himself would one day come to earth and give His life to bring man and God back together again.

And then Meshach watched as his father carried the bowl of blood to the door of their home. Eli took a sprig of hyssop, dipped it into the bowl of blood, and splashed some of the blood on the two doorposts. Then he splashed some on the door jamb above the door too. The whole thing was messy with blood everywhere, but Meshach knew they must do it. They must obey. It was the only way to be safe from the tenth plague of death.

Meshach looked at the dead lamb. The meat would now be taken to the cooking fire to be roasted so that they could eat it. The skin and bones were to be offered on an altar as a burning sacrifice. As the smoke from the sacrifice floated up into evening sky, Meshach tried to explain the whole thing to Seti, but it was hard. How do you explain the death of God for man?

It was hard enough for a Hebrew to understand, let alone an Egyptian. Seti's gods would never give their lives for him! They couldn't, even if they did exist! Only the Creator could pay the price for sinful people!

The twilight had settled, and everyone was gathering in their homes to eat the Passover meal. All up and down the narrow street in front of Meshach's house, he could see the neighbors going into their homes. And there was blood splashed on every doorpost to protect them against the plague.

Meshach felt strange as he gathered with his family in the one small room of their own mud-brick home. Everyone was there—Meshach, Seti, Chilion, Kezia, Mother, Father, and Seti's mother.

They ate the roasted lamb and the bitter herbs with it. They broke the flat bread and passed it around the family circle. Everything for the meal had been prepared just as Moses had said it should be. The special directions for the meal had come from Jehovah Himself.

Meshach shivered again in spite of the warm evening. The whole thing was all so exciting, and yet so frightening. Would any of the Hebrew firstborn die tonight? If they had failed to put blood on their doorposts, he knew the answer was Yes. Like the Egyptians, they would be without an excuse. Over and over again Moses had warned them about that.

Everyone had finished the meal now, and Meshach noticed the family was standing around as though they were ready to leave at any moment. No one had bothered to sit down. Meshach knew they were all waiting for word from Joshua and Caleb. When it was time to leave, the two leaders would blow rams' horns to make the announcement.

The hours seemed to drag by as everyone waited. A round orange moon rose over the eastern horizon and then slowly climbed its way up into the heavens. To Meshach, this night looked like any other. Insects chirped from their hideouts; nighthawks screeched as they swooped the night sky in search of their evening meal. The desert wind whistled and moaned as it wandered its way down the narrow streets of Goshen.

Meshach didn't go up to the rooftop to sleep. He didn't even lie down by the charcoal oven to rest for a while. As the night deepened, he just stood in the open doorway, waiting for something, anything, to break the spell of dread he was beginning to feel.

What if the blood on the doorpost wasn't enough to protect their home from the final plague of death? What if Moses had missed telling them something they needed to know about getting ready for the plague? What if Jehovah couldn't be trusted to keep His word?

Meshach looked at his father. There was a look of peace on Eli's face as though he hadn't a care in the world. But it was Kezia Meshach was worried about most. She stood leaning against the wall, her head drooping from the long wait. He knew she was worried. After all, her life was at stake.

Suddenly Meshach felt bad about the doubts that he had allowed to creep into his mind. He walked across the room to stand by her. "Don't worry, Sister," he assured her. "Jehovah has been good to us. Not only has he saved us from the last six plagues, He's told us what to do to escape this final plague."

Kezia didn't say anything. She only squeezed Meshach's hand as if to thank him for his words of comfort.

And then at midnight the plague came. Suddenly Meshach could hear wailing, faintly at first, but then louder and more pitiful. It sounded as if people were screaming in anguish—the way they did when they were mourning at the funeral of a loved one. Meshach hoped the wailing wasn't coming from Hebrew homes. Surely every Hebrew family in the settlement where Meshach lived had put blood on their doorposts.

Maybe the sounds came from the homes of the Egyptian slave overseers, or maybe from the Egyptian officers in charge of the building projects. They lived right there in Goshen. Their homes were nicer than the average Hebrew homes, and they lived in their own little section of town with walls around their estates, but they did live in Goshen. They needed to be in Goshen to make sure the Hebrew men were getting to their work assignments every day.

And now more people could be heard wailing. Lots of them! The eerie sounds came drifting on the night air like waves of smoke. Meshach rushed to the door of their house, but his father held him back and kept him from going out into the street. "Let it be, Meshach," he said quietly. "There's nothing we can do." Eli's eyes looked sad in the dim light of the clay oil lamps.

And Meshach knew his father was right. The day of mercy had passed. Pharaoh had been given ten chances to see that Jehovah was serious when

He said, "Let My people go!" All Egypt had been given the opportunity to see the power of the One True God. They could have come to Goshen like Seti and his mother did to learn about Jehovah's mysterious ways. They could be resting right now inside the walls of a Hebrew home, safe from this one final terrible plague that had come upon Egypt.

The wailing grew louder as more and more Egyptian families realized they had lost their firstborns. From far and near the sounds came, and Meshach finally had to cover his ears to keep out the sound of it.

Meshach watched as Seti's mother hugged him close. There was terror in Amena's eyes as though she feared she might lose him any moment. He was her firstborn and her only child. Seti looked scared too, but as the moments ticked by and nothing happened, the two of them began to relax. And then finally Amena began to cry softly.

Later Seti joined Meshach where he stood looking out through the open doorway. "Praise be to Jehovah," Seti said softly as he hung his head. "At first I wasn't sure that the words you told me were true, Meshach. You said that Jehovah is God—your God—the One and Only Invisible God of heaven and earth. Remember? It was that day in the storeroom when we almost had a fight."

Meshach nodded. He remembered the day very well.

"And then you said you wished that I could know Him like you do." Meshach could see Seti's face in the bright moonlight. His expression was solemn, but there was a look of peace on his face too. Meshach could tell that this was probably the most important moment of Seti's life—the moment when he fully realized that Jehovah was the One True God.

Seti nodded his head slowly. "You spoke as if you really knew your God, and you made me want to believe in Him too, even if I couldn't see Him. And, Meshach, now I believe the rest of what you said, too. I guess I knew it all along." Seti hung his head again. "Your God will set you and your people free."

It was long past midnight now as the two boys stood talking. "Thank you for being merciful to Mother and me the way the One True God is merciful." Seti gave a deep sigh of relief. "My mother and I are safe at last."

CHAPTER 32

A sound of running footsteps sounded in the night. Meshach stirred where he was dozing fitfully. He had finally allowed himself to sit down on the floor by the front door. Seti was sleeping too where he sat beside Meshach.

Who could be running down the street at this time of night? Meshach wondered. And who would want to, with the tenth and final plague upon all Egypt?

To Meshach's surprise the footsteps slowed and then stopped at the front door of their house. Meshach scrambled to his feet as a voice called out. "Eli, from the house of Uzziel? Aaron has asked that Meshach come at once!"

In an instant Eli was at the front door. "What's the matter?" he asked anxiously. "Is something wrong?"

"Pharaoh Amenhotep is calling for Moses, but—the way is dark, and—" The messenger tried to catch his breath. "And Moses wishes to take a final gift to the Pharaoh—he needs someone to go with him to the palace!"

"And he's calling for Meshach?" Eli stepped toward the door. "Does Aaron want me to come too? Just give me a few moments to get ready."

"No!" The man was still out of breath. "He said that you are to remain inside your home. You are a firstborn, and the plague is still upon us."

Meshach's heart began to race. The great and powerful Moses was asking for him! But what about Joshua and Caleb? Why weren't they being called to go?

Almost in answer to Meshach's thoughts, the messenger said, "Joshua and Caleb can't go! They are both firstborn, and Aaron can't go either! He needs to have a final council with the head elders. Moses has said that we'll all be leaving Egypt before sunup!"

Eli turned to Meshach, now wide awake. "Put your sandals on, Son, and go with the messenger!" He laid his hand on Meshach's shoulder. "And be careful," he added solemnly.

Meshach grinned in the darkness. In a flash he was out the door—he already had his sandals on—everybody had their sandals on—it was one of the commands that Moses had given the Hebrews in Goshen before this horrible night had begun.

Meshach raced up the darkened street. The moon was in the western sky now, making long shadows in every alley and lane of the Goshen settlement. In shorter time than in takes to tell, Meshach was at Aaron's doorstep. Moses was already there.

When he saw Meshach come in the door, he smiled tiredly. "Now, that was fast! I guess I should have expected as much, though." He handed Meshach a basket to carry on his head and a lighted torch. As Meshach put the basket on his head, he noticed that it was filled with all kinds of delicacies. Almonds and pistachio nuts and small clay jars. The jars probably had myrrh and spices in them. Maybe balm. Or else honey. These were common gifts to give when one was going to visit someone important.

In a matter of minutes they were out the door and on their way to the capital city. Meshach had never been alone in the presence of Moses. He had never even imagined that such a thing would happen. Meshach, son of Eli, a common baker and scribe. Out on the darkened streets of Goshen, walking with the most important man in all of Egypt!

Meshach didn't know what to say, so he said nothing. The two of them walked along in silence for quite some time. It was as if they were both deeply absorbed in their own thoughts, awed by the events of the day.

But finally Meshach knew he had to say something. It was too great of a moment to let slip away. He might not ever get the chance again to speak with Moses like this.

"Do you think Pharaoh will really let us go this time?" Meshach was scared to talk with the great man, but he tried to keep himself calm.

"He'll let us go now—there's nothing else he can do. He has nothing left to bargain with. Even his son, the crown prince, is dead now." Moses sighed as though a great sadness had come over him. "The only thing left would be for Amenhotep himself to die, and I'm sure by now, he must be feeling like that would not be such a bad thing." Moses shook his head. "He can't be very popular in Egypt right now."

Meshach looked up at the tall man striding beside him down the road to Tanis. It was the dead of night. The torch Meshach carried sent wisps of sooty smoke curling upward as they walked along. All around them shadows danced in weird shapes like giants looming in the darkness.

"Please tell me," Meshach grew more bold, "what's it like to have Jehovah really speak to you? I mean—what does His voice sound like? Did you see Him? My father told me that He spoke to you from a burning bush."

Meshach had been wanting to ask these questions of Moses for a long time now. Some of them he had been wondering about ever since that first day he had seen Moses and Aaron in the royal court when they asked Pharaoh to let the slaves go free.

Moses put his arm on Meshach's shoulder as they walked along. "Well, let's see. The voice of the Almighty is deep and strong—and yet it's kind and compassionate." Meshach could feel Moses smiling at him in the darkness.

"I'll never forget the way His voice sounded the first time I heard it. I was standing there with my sheep, just staring at that bush. It was the most amazing thing I've ever seen. The bush was burning with bright flames that never went out, and it made me feel warm and safe somehow. I knew that Jehovah was in the bush, before He even spoke. I could feel His goodness, and the place seemed holy. I finally fell to my knees, and I just felt that I wanted to stay there forever!" Meshach thought he could hear Moses' voice tremble as he said the words.

The great man smiled in the light of the torch. "It's hard to explain, Meshach. You would have to have been there to completely understand, I guess. Maybe someday Jehovah will speak to you. And maybe one day you'll be a leader in Israel and speak for Jehovah too."

A lump formed in Meshach's throat. The very idea of such a thing filled him with awe. He couldn't speak. He could hardly breathe at the thought of it all.

The trip to the palace went by quickly—more quickly than Meshach had thought possible. It was if they had wings on their feet. In some ways, Meshach could hardly wait to go inside the palace and see all the wonders for himself. At the same time, he just wanted to continue walking along beside Moses. It was a wonderful feeling for Meshach to be with Moses, and he knew he would never forget this night for as long as he lived.

But what would happen when they arrived at the palace? Would Pharaoh have one of his temper tantrums when they got there? Would he get mad and order that the two of them be executed?

Meshach guessed he wasn't too worried about that right now. The way things were going lately, Moses had all the power, and Pharaoh Amenhotep knew it. And besides, Jehovah wouldn't let anything happen to them even if Amenhotep did try something.

The big bronze gates swung slowly open, and Meshach and Moses stepped through them into the royal courtyard. No one tried to stop Meshach this time. Besides the two guards standing guard at the gate, no one else was around.

Meshach wondered how many firstborn there were in the royal family. He could hear pitiful wails on the night air as he and Moses walked down the corridors toward the royal courtroom. The voices of the mourners sounded eerie, and Meshach moved closer to Moses.

And then suddenly they were standing at the giant mahogany doors to the royal courtroom. Meshach had never seen the large room from this angle. He had only seen it from above. When he was down below, the columns looked much taller—the narrow turquoise carpet to the throne appeared much longer.

Far ahead at the end of the narrow carpet sat Pharaoh on his throne. His hands gripped the armrests of his throne and his knees were shaking. As Moses and Meshach silently approached the throne, Meshach could see Amenhotep's jaw trembling. They stood for several moments waiting for

Amenhotep to speak, and when he finally did, Meshach thought it was the saddest thing he had ever heard.

"I have sinned!" his voice quavered. "I have sinned before Jehovah, and now because of my stubborn pride, my son is dead." Pharaoh's shoulders shook as he bowed his head in grief and wept silently.

After some time he finally spoke again. "I was wrong not to listen to you!" he continued, his head still bowed. "Jehovah is Lord of all heaven and earth as you said, and there is none like Him!" The Pharaoh swallowed hard as he raised his head to look at Moses. A great battle seemed to be raging in his mind, but he spoke with conviction.

"Go now! Go at once! Please leave or all Egypt will be destroyed!" Pharaoh Amenhotep raised his arm and pointed toward the tall doors to the courtroom. "Leave now before I change my mind again! Go serve your God! Take your flocks and herds and your families with you!"

CHAPTER 33

Moses hadn't spoken a word since he and Meshach had entered the courtroom, and now it seemed that there was still nothing to say. He slowly turned to go, and Meshach with him.

"Wait!" the Pharaoh begged.

Meshach and Moses turned in time to see Pharaoh Amenhotep fall to his knees in front of his throne.

"Please! I can't let you go without asking a blessing from you! Please!" The great man lifted his hands as if to plead his case. "Do you have even one blessing that you can give me?"

There were tears in the great ruler's eyes, and he didn't even try to wipe them away.

Moses turned to the throne again and bowed slightly. "May the Lord God of Abraham, Isaac, and Jacob have mercy on you and your people." Moses was quick and to the point. "May you and your people learn from the lesson that Jehovah has tried to teach you—that He is the source of all life and blessing and that there is no other God like Him in heaven or earth."

Then they left. The last thing Meshach saw as they turned to go was the gold and ivory of the royal throne gleaming and glittering in the light of the midnight torches. And there on the floor in front of the throne was the mighty Pharaoh kneeling, his face in his hands.

The trip home seemed to take forever. Meshach was so excited, he could hardly keep himself from running, but he did because he wanted to be able to walk and talk with Moses one last time.

And Moses shared with him many things. He told him all the stories about God's plan to set them free and take them all to Canaan. He talked about how good it would be to live in the land of milk and honey, where they could build their own houses and grow their own crops. And of course they would be free to worship Jehovah as they pleased.

Meshach knew he would never forget the talk that he and Moses had that night. As the two of them finally neared the settlement in Goshen where they lived, Moses laid a hand on Meshach's shoulder. "Meshach, my son," the great leader said softly, "if you are faithful to Jehovah, I am sure He will one day do great things through you too." It made Meshach shiver with delight just thinking about it.

By the time they arrived back in Goshen, the hour was late. It was so late, in fact, that it was actually early—before long the sun would be up. The first faint colors of dawn were beginning to light the eastern horizon.

Meshach wasn't surprised at the sight that greeted his eyes as they came up the narrow street in front of his house. All the neighbors were scurrying around loading their belongings on carts and pack animals. Some were hitching their oxen to two-wheeled carts. Some were tying big bundles on the backs of donkeys. Others were going to just carry everything on their shoulders and on top of their heads.

Flocks of goats and sheep were milling about, and herd boys with their little dogs were trying to keep them from getting way. Some families had a few head of cattle, and a few even had a camel, but these were the exception. Most were too poor to own such animals.

But at a time like this no one seemed to care about how much someone else might have. They were on their way out of Egypt.

Meshach grabbed Seti by the shoulder, and the two of them danced around in a circle in the busy street. "We're going to Canaan! We're going to Canaan!" Meshach shouted. "We'll live like kings and eat milk and honey!"

"And your family will be free!" Seti shouted back. His eyes were shining as if this were the best day of his life, too. And it truly was. He and his mother were leaving behind a life of pagan superstition. Now they were on their way to a new life with God's people.

When the boys settled down a bit, Meshach helped Seti load their ox cart with the few things they would be taking along. First came the large wooden box filled with the valuable things the Egyptians had given them. It was the first time Meshach had seen the jewelry, gold, and silver together in one place. He was surprised at how much there was. The weight of all the precious metals and jewels was so heavy that it was hard to lift the box.

"Father, the Lord has been good to us." Meshach bowed his head reverently. "We should give an offering to the Lord to show how grateful we are."

"That's a good idea, Son. I'm sure we'll have a chance to do that once we get out of Egypt or when we get settled in Canaan."

The two boys loaded other things the family would need into the cart—clay pots, the kneading trough for making bread, and baskets of grain, lentils, and onions. Next came lighter things like goat-hair blankets and any clothes they weren't wearing.

Meshach was tired. Except for a couple short naps, he had been awake all night.

"Why don't you climb up on top of the cart and rest." Eli smiled at Meshach as the three of them tied the load down snugly. "The other family members can walk for now. They haven't been up all night doing Jehovah's business like you have."

Meshach climbed up onto the cart and gave a tired sigh. It was good to rest finally, but he didn't want to sleep just yet. There was too much going on, and he didn't want to miss anything.

A ram's horn sounded somewhere in the distance, and then suddenly the cart began to move. As it bumped along, Meshach looked out over the stream of people pouring up the street. The night of tragedy for Egypt had ended in a new dawn for the Hebrews. Meshach and his people were finally leaving Egypt. It was actually happening! The years of slavery were over.

It was time to say goodbye to the old life. It was time to say goodbye to the overseers and their cruel whips. It was time to say goodbye to Pharaoh.

Pharaoh Amenhotep had missed his chances to let the Hebrews leave when there was still something for them to leave behind. Now most of the livestock in Egypt were dead from disease. The hailstorm had destroyed all the crops in Egypt, and anything that was left had been eaten up by the locusts. And worst of all, the firstborn of Egypt were all dead. Every household had suffered the loss of someone.

Pharaoh Amenhotep had been given ten chances to see the truth about the Hebrews—that they were Jehovah's chosen people set aside to become a great nation. Ten times Pharaoh had been warned to let them go. Ten times he had refused. Ten times Jehovah's plagues had hit the land of Egypt.

Meshach shook his head sadly. Lord Amenhotep hadn't been wise at all. He had definitely underestimated the power of Jehovah. If the whole thing hadn't been so terrible, Meshach might have been tempted to—well—there was no sense in gloating over the way things had turned out for Pharaoh Amenhotep.

Meshach smiled, a tired grin on his face as the cart bumped its way out of the Hebrew settlement and into the wide-open grasslands of Goshen. "I guess we can say this has been ten ways to say goodbye to Pharaoh." He sighed. "It's just too bad that Pharaoh didn't say goodbye the first time and then be done with it. Now he has to say goodbye anyway, but he's got nothing left to show for it."

The sky was turning pink now as daybreak approached, and songbirds were singing a springtime tune. Around him Meshach could see a whole sea of people and animals moving east. The whole thing was almost too exciting for words.

Behind them lay Egypt—ahead of them lay Canaan. With rams' horns blowing, goats bleating, and old men singing, Meshach and his people were on their way to a new life. They were finally on their way to the land of milk and honey.

IF YOU ENJOYED THIS BOOK, YOU'LL WANT TO READ THESE, TOO!

Summer of the Sharks
Sally Streib

Twelve-year-old Eric and his twin sister, Susan, go with their Aunt Sally on a diving expedition in the Caribbean. One problem—Eric is afraid to dive! Find out how God helps him overcome his fears, and how He can help you with your fears, too!

Paperback. 128 pages. 0-8163-2126-4. US$7.99, Can$11.99

The Great Sleepy-Time Stew Rescue (an Honors Club story)
Charles Mills

Alex Timmons decides to take up cooking. His soup is awful, but it comes in handy when he and his friends need to escape from kidnappers. Clues for earning the Pathfinder Cooking honor are included.

Paperback. 128 pages. 0-8163-2009-8. US$7.99, Can$11.99

Wings Over Oshkosh (an Honors Club story)
Charles Mills

Jackie Anderson is mad at everybody and everything. Her parents are in jail, a bully in school is making her life miserable, and an airplane nearly crashes into her. Find clues for earning the Pathfinder Airplane Modeling honor in this one-of-a-kind thriller.

Paperback. 128 pages. 0-8163-2089-6. US$7.99, Can$11.99

Order from your ABC by calling **1-800-765-6955**, or get online and shop our virtual store at <**www.AdventistBookCenter.com**>.
• Read a chapter from your favorite book
• Order online
• Sign up for email notices on new products